The ADOPTION CLUB

Barbara Scott

Waterford, Virginia

The Adoption Club

Published in the U.S. by: **OakTara Publishers**
P.O. Box 8, Waterford, VA 20197
www.oaktara.com

Cover design by David LaPlaca/debest design co.
Cover illustration © 2009, Barbara Scott
Author photo © 2009 by Gary H. Scott

Copyright © 2009 by Barbara Scott. All rights reserved.

Scripture is taken from the King James Version of the Bible.

ISBN: 978-1-60290-118-6

The Adoption Club is a work of fiction. References to real people, events, establishments, organizations, or locales are intended only to provide a sense of authenticity and are used fictitiously. All other characters, incidents, and dialogue are drawn from the author's imagination.

Printed in the U.S.A.

To all who have been adopted

To those who have struggled with being adopted
and those who know inherently that their lives
were blessed with the adoption.

To those who found each other, formed "adoption clubs,"
and supported each other along the journey.

To those who found their true identity,
quite separate from their birth parents
or their adoptive parents,
but in Abba Father.

Acknowledgments

A huge thank you to my mother, who is the model for the main fictional character. She shared her journey and was open about the internal struggles that a lot of adopted people keep secret.

Thank you to my sisters, Kathryn and Dianne. Although you may not totally understand or agree, you have been extremely supportive and encouraging of my writing.

Thank you to Gary for being my loving husband and biggest fan for over 37 years. With you by my side I'll go on to write many more books that are locked up in my head.

Thank you to Justin, Nathan, and Bethany, my dear family, for once again rooting me on.

Thank you to Brock and Bodie Thoene for your Writers' Workshops, which I took in Kona, Hawaii, several years ago. You gave me the foundation and inspiration to write fiction as well as nonfiction.

Thank you to the writers' group at Youth With A Mission's University of the Nations for your weekly critiques, prayers, and loving encouragement. Now that I live far away from you, I can't believe how hard it is to write a book without you. We became more than a writers' group as we supported each other through life's good and hard times.

Thank you, Sandi Tompkins, not only for facilitating the writers' group, but for pushing me to get my proposal done before I moved off the big island of Hawaii. You are the gel that holds the writers' group together because your love for each one gives the confidence that we can succeed.

Thank you to my dear friend Suzanne Field, mother of two adopted children, who spent precious hours of her personal time proofing, editing, and reworking the rough edges into a polished manuscript.

Thank you to my publishers, OakTara, with a special thanks to Ramona Tucker, whose own adopted daughter was very ill at the time I submitted my proposal. Yet you found time to read my manuscript.

Above all, thank you to my Lord God, the Great Author, who helped me write this book. May it cause us all to want to be in *The Adoption Club* so we, too, can cry, "Abba Father."

One

The Orphanage

I was six years old. The cold wind blew leaves across the lawn the night Mrs. McMillan brought my ten-year-old brother, Harold, and me to the orphanage. We had been taken away from our mother before and placed in foster homes, but somehow this felt different.

"What's this big place?" I whispered to Harold.

"Shhh. Just do what Mrs. McMillan tells you to do."

I began crying. "I'm scared."

"Don't worry. I'll be here if you need me," assured my brother.

"But we've always been together when we were at foster homes—we could play."

"We're still together. I'll just be in a building for boys and you'll be with the girls. You'll be okay."

I wiped away the tears and hoped the other girls wouldn't notice I'd been crying.

An older boy met us, and Mrs. McMillan instructed him to show Harold where he was going to stay.

Mrs. McMillan had been nice the other times she had taken us to foster homes, but I was still a little afraid of her. New homes were always scary, and this one was really big with lots of girls and boys who made me feel shy.

We were met by the matron, Miss Paige, whose perfume was so heavy I felt dizzy. An older woman, slightly plump, with gray hair pulled back into a tight bun, Miss Paige wore a plain black dress with black, heavy looking shoes.

"Bernice, this is Miss Paige. She will show you where to go and introduce you to the girls," said Mrs. McMillan.

Miss Paige gave me a slight nod.

"Well, then, I'll be on my way." Mrs. McMillan gave me a little pat on the back before leaving.

"Follow me," said Miss Paige as she turned and marched into the girls' dormitory. I felt a lump in my throat, but I was trying not to cry.

When we first walked into the dormitory the girls were playing noisily, but stopped what they were doing when they noticed Miss Paige standing inside the door. It became very quiet.

"Girls, this is Bernice. She has come to live here. Elsie, she will share a bed with you. Can you show her around?"

"Yes, ma'am." Elsie's red curls bobbed as she nodded.

"Those of you in first grade, please make her feel welcome. Can you all say hello to Bernice?"

"Hello, Bernice," the girls called out in unison.

"Bernice, come to breakfast with Elsie in the morning," Miss Paige instructed. "Then I will take you to the classroom and introduce you to your teacher."

I nodded.

"Good night, then. Lights out in fifteen minutes," commanded Miss Paige as she turned and walked out.

Although there were lots of girls looking at me, I felt very alone. While the girls went back to reading, talking, or playing in groups I shuffled my feet and stared at the floor. Slowly I looked up and around.

White wrought-iron single beds lined both walls of the long room with a white chenille bedspread pulled tightly and a pillow placed at the head of each one. Beautiful wood floors were waxed to a shine. The crisp smell of bleach, detergent, and floor wax permeated the air. There were only a few windows up high, but it was dark out anyhow.

It never smelled like this at our house. Somehow the odors make it seem very clean.

Slowly I made my way over to the bed where Elsie was playing with a rag doll.

"Hi," Elsie said sweetly. "Do you have a nickname? I could call you 'Bernie.'"

"No, just call me Bernice."

"Okay."

The girls were all in matching cream-colored muslin nightgowns covered with patches. Elsie grabbed one from a basket in the corner and tossed it to me.

I didn't know then that the children never got the same clothes back after laundry day. Sometimes clothing would be too large, and sometimes it was too small. No one had personal belongings. Everything was shared.

"Put your nightgown on in the bathroom over there."

The bathroom was large and just as clean as the other room with ten sinks, ten stalls, and ten bathtubs all shared by about fifty girls. Black-and-white-checkered ceramic tiles were chipped in the corners but made the floor look like a giant checkerboard. The smell of Pine Sol was strong there, too. It was probably the most sterile place I had ever been in.

I hurried out of my clothes and into the nightgown. Once back in the large sleeping quarters, I sat down on the bed next to Elsie. "Umm. Where do I put my clothes?"

"We each have a cubby. Come, I'll show you," said Elsie as she led the way to a room filled with very small closets.

I opened the door to my cubby. There was a shelf on top for books or a toy, and a place to hang clothes. I placed my shoes on the bottom.

"Tomorrow they'll give you a school uniform. I'll be in the same class as you. We have a mean teacher named Mrs. Conoway. Wanna play with my doll?"

"Okay," I said, following Elsie.

We both climbed up on the bed.

"Does everyone else have a bed of their own?" I inquired.

"No. It's just so it looks nice for visitors to see. We're not even allowed to use the pillows. At night we stack them over there in the corner. There's two or three girls in each bed. We share a bed with Martha. Sleep up here next to me. I make her sleep at the other end because sometimes she wets the bed."

"Yuck. Do you like it here?" I asked.

Elsie shrugged. "It's okay. You'll get used to it. At least we get three meals a day and a warm place to sleep."

"Do you have a mom?"

"No, she died," said Elsie as she looked down at her rag doll. "I remember my dad a little. But the last time I saw him was a long time ago. He was always asleep on the couch. How 'bout you?"

"I had different daddies. The one I liked the most was knitting me mittens."

"Really?" exclaimed Elsie. "I never heard of a daddy knitting."

"Yeah, then all of the sudden one day the police broke in to our house and charged down to our basement. I heard glass breaking, and a funny smell came from the basement. I had noticed that smell before, but not so strong. The police took him away in handcuffs. I was crying. My mommy said the police broke something called a 'still.' I guess that Daddy made booze in it. Then he had to go to jail 'cuz for some reason the police don't let people make their own booze."

"What about your mommy?"

"She'll probably come to get my brother, Harold, and me soon. We've been in foster homes before, and she always comes to get us after a while or Mrs. McMillan takes us back home."

"Don't count on it," Elsie said, shaking her red curls. "When they put you here, it's because your mom signed some papers giving you to the orphanage."

The tears couldn't be held back any longer; the floodgates opened. "I want my brother," I sobbed as I wrapped my arms around my middle, rocking back and forth.

Several older girls gathered around us.

"Don't cry, kid," said a girl of about fourteen. "We've all gone through it. You'll learn to 'buck up.' Once in a while someone gets adopted. Keep thinking about that. It gives you a little hope."

"What's 'adopted'?"

"Sometimes people who don't have kids want a little boy or girl. It doesn't happen very often, but sometimes they come here and pick out a kid and take them home. You get to stay there for good."

"How do you know if they'll be nice?"

"If they wanted a kid bad enough to adopt one, they'd probably be nice."

That made sense to me.

I fit into life in the orphanage and time slipped by. Nearly two years would pass before my life would take another turn.

Two

Turning Point

The matron, Miss Paige, was talking to Anna, one of the older girls, when I heard my name.

"Bernice is wanted at the main office right away. Anna, wash her hands and face, comb her hair, and put a clean uniform on her. This is probably her last chance."

What did she mean "last chance?" Last chance for what? I wondered. Besides, I knew I hadn't done anything wrong, and the matron was smiling. The children weren't sent to the office for wrongdoing. They were punished on the spot.

"Okay, come on." Anna took me by the hand. "I hope this works out for you. No such luck for me."

"Why?"

"I'm too old."

Why is Anna too old and I'm not? I couldn't help thinking.

Besides, I had not been in the office since I arrived, and that seemed a long time ago. But I didn't ask any more questions. I had learned older people didn't like little kids asking questions, especially if they didn't know the answers.

Soon I was washed, combed, dressed in a clean uniform, and stood in front of a mirror.

"Well, what do you think?" asked Anna.

As I peered in the mirror, I didn't see anything special. All the girls had the same basic haircut—just below the ears cut straight around. My eyes were hazel; my hair was light brown and a little wavy. The previous year Mrs. Conoway, our teacher, had told me I looked like Amelia Earhart, a famous woman pilot, who had just flown across the Atlantic Ocean. Mrs. Conoway showed me a picture and I did see a resemblance. *Wouldn't it be wonderful to grow up and do something great like Amelia Earhart?* I daydreamed.

"Okay, enough with the inspection," said Anna as she sent me on my way with instructions to "be good."

We girls walked behind the main office three times a day as we marched double file to the dining hall, so I knew where I was being summoned, although children were not usually allowed in that building.

It was spring, and the sun felt warm. I wasn't sure just how long I had been in the orphanage. It had been cold when my brother and I had been brought here. I had been in the first grade then and now was in second grade. I remembered two Christmases and a Fourth of July. It seemed a very long time.

I walked around to the front of the main office building and climbed the wide stone steps. The great front door was hard to open because it was heavy and the big brass knob was hard to turn. I managed to slip in before the door closed again. It seemed dark inside with a thick, patterned rug surrounded by a shiny, varnished wood floor. The walls were beige and the tall windows and doors were framed in dark oak. Heavy burgundy velvet drapes let in little light.

In a moment my eyes became adjusted to the dimness and I saw a lady behind the desk.

"Hello. You must be Bernice. Some people want to meet you," she said. She was smiling as though she had a secret, but I didn't ask any questions. It was so quiet in this large place. In all my time at the orphanage I hadn't been away from the other girls.

"Go through that door," said the lady, pointing. "Mrs. McMillan is there. You remember her."

I wasn't sure if that was a question, so I nodded and moved in the direction the receptionist indicated. My stomach churned with mixed-up feelings, and my heart pounded.

Who wants to see me? I wondered, trembling a little. The only people I knew were the matrons, the teachers, and a few other people who worked here. The cluster of brownstone buildings had been my whole world for quite a while. My feet felt like lead as I walked slower and slower. Then, passing through the huge double doors, I stood still. The three people in the large sitting room hadn't seen me yet.

Mrs. McMillan was talking. "Her mother tried, but it's hard to manage in these hard times. Her husband deserted her, and women don't get paid enough to take care of a family, if they can find work at all. We hate to separate the children, but it seems the best thing to do. The mother still has the baby and the boy will soon be old enough to go out and find work, so her mother recently agreed to let Bernice be adopted if we could find her a good home. She is eight years old, born December 1, 1921, and...Oh, Bernice, come in, dear. These people would like to meet you."

I felt small and alone in this large room with three grown-ups looking at me. *I wish some of the older girls were here with me.*

There were so many questions flying around in my head. *Why did my mother agree to adoption? Isn't she ever coming back? Doesn't she love me? Are they going to take me away from my brother, too?*

Then I noticed the people were all smiling. That gave me courage. Still I thought, *I have gone to foster homes before and I hadn't been inspected ahead of time; I had just been delivered.*

I took a few steps forward. There was a man and a woman with Mrs. McMillan. The man seemed tall sitting in a large leather chair. His hair was thin and gray as was his small mustache. He had bushy eyebrows above his deep-set gray eyes, which were warm and friendly. He wore a dark suit with a stiff-collared white shirt and a dark red tie. His large hands rested on the arms of the chair. They looked like calloused working hands, but very clean. His long legs were crossed, and his black ankle-high shoes were polished to a shine.

The woman looked friendly, too. An abundance of gray hair was piled on top of her head in soft curls with a hair net to keep it neat. A pretty straw hat with flowers sat in her lap. She had a soft-looking navy and white dress under a lightweight navy coat. A large leather handbag sat beside her on the floor, and a pair of gloves was clasped in one hand. The lady wore silk stockings and black shoes with a strap that buttoned on one side. She sat on the edge of her chair as though wanting to come to greet me.

Feelings that were very new began to stir inside of me. When I was young I had been told that little kids were a lot of trouble to take care of. No one had ever been anxious to meet me before.

Why are these people interested in me? Could it be these people want a little girl? I had heard of such a thing. But of the one hundred or so girls in my building, only two I knew of had left before they were sixteen years old.

I moved slowly around toward Mrs. McMillan. She seemed at least a little familiar because she was the "welfare lady" who brought me here. After that I had seen Mrs. McMillan only occasionally from a distance.

"I want you to meet Mr. and Mrs. Nesbitt. They are looking for a little girl to come live with them. Would you like that?" Mrs. McMillan asked.

I was tongue-tied. *Could it be they really want me? For keeps? No one's ever wanted me before. What if they get tired of me after a while and send me back?*

Foster homes hadn't kept me. But this time, something felt different. I nodded.

"We live on a big farm with cows, horses, cats, and a dog," Mr. Nesbitt leaned forward, as though trying to impress me.

He wants me to like him. I had strange feelings I didn't know how to identify.

Mrs. Nesbitt said, "Yes, and you will have a room of your own and pretty clothes."

She's doing it too. I looked from one to the other and then at Mrs. McMillan, who was smiling and gave a slight nod.

Suddenly, my stomach did a little flip. My breath caught in my throat and a big smile came from somewhere deep inside. I wanted to jump up and down and clap my hands.

They want me. They really want me!

A dream was coming true. The girls had talked about being adopted—had fantasized about someone coming and taking them away from here, but I had thought there was little chance of such a thing...until now.

"Have we reached an agreement?" asked Mrs. McMillan. "Or would you like to see some other girls?"

Oh, please no. I felt my heart sink. *They may choose someone else. Elsie's hair is curly, too, and her teeth are straighter than mine.*

"I think Bernice is the right one," said Mrs. Nesbitt, glancing at her husband.

He gave her a quick nod and smiled.

"It's settled then. It will take some time to do the paperwork. I'll bring her to you in a week. Bernice, you may go back to your dormitory now." Mrs. McMillan gave a little wave of dismissal.

I wanted to stay with these people. In fact, I wanted to go with them right away. But I had been trained to obey commands and never talk to grown-ups unless spoken to. I did a little skip, then walked quickly out the big doors and across the rug in front of the receptionist's desk. The lady at the desk didn't speak but flashed me that little secret smile and waved.

Then I stepped out into the sunshine.

Three

The Big Day

Out in the spring sunshine, there was no need to hurry back to my dormitory. No one would miss me for awhile. I needed time to think about all that had just happened before being peppered with questions from all the girls.

I looked around at all the brownstone buildings. The main office was part of the building that contained the kitchen, dining room, and an auditorium. Then there was the building for babies and little children and another for boys. My brother was there, but I rarely had a chance to talk with him. Sometimes I saw him when we walked to the dining room.

Will I ever see him again? I want to go live with the Nesbitts, but what will Harold think of me for leaving him? I guess he doesn't need me, but I will miss him.

There was also a school and a hospital. I had been in the hospital once when I had the mumps. Church services and Sunday school were held in the school building.

This had been home for two years. *What will my new life be like? Will there be any other children nearby to play with?*

Building five, the girls' dorm, was a large three-storied building with a tower on one corner. The basement was where we girls spent most of our time. The big girls scrubbed the wood floors every Saturday. The walls were painted brown to hide the marks from the straight chairs that lined the walls. Each girl was assigned a chair and that was her only personal space.

Did Mrs. Nesbitt really say I would have a whole room of my own? I never had a room of my own, even in a foster home.

The first floor of building five was a huge living room with polished wooden floors and heavy furniture. A large fern stood on a pedestal in the tower room. The living room looked very nice, but we girls were never allowed there except to walk single file from the basement to the second or third floor, barefoot on our way to bed. Most of the second floor was a large room lined with narrow wrought-iron beds. The big girls made beds every day. They helped us bathe every Saturday night. Two at a time, and no playing! Every Saturday evening we were assigned clean clothes, long black stockings, and nighties for the week. Since nothing was our own except our shoes and toothbrush, we often had a dress too long or too short.

Did Mrs. Nesbitt really say I would have pretty clothes?

The third floor had beds too, but no bathtubs in their bathroom. Most of the older girls slept up there. The tower room was closed off to make a sewing room for Mrs. White, who came every Wednesday to mend clothes. Once I had been sent there with something for her to mend and she allowed me to stay for awhile. She was putting new elastic in bloomers. She fastened a length of elastic on a safety pin and allowed me to push it through the casing. Then she sewed the ends of the elastic together. After that day she always sent for me when she was doing elastic. She was the only adult that took notice of me until now, and that was the beginning of my love for sewing.

Now more questions began to form in my head. *Why do they want me? What is it going to be like to live on a farm?* I had always lived in a city before I came here. *Where would I go to school? I wouldn't know anyone.*

They want me! But what if they change their minds? Who

13

decided to send for me? It must have been Mrs. McMillan. Why didn't they take a baby? There are lots of babies. And why didn't they want Harold? They want ME! They WANT me! THEY WANT ME!!!

I had nearly stopped walking when the big bell above the dining hall brought me back to the present. That was the first dinner bell. I hurried down the steps to the basement, where the girls were all sitting in their chairs with arms folded while two older girls were going from one to another combing hair. When the second bell rang we marched to the dining hall.

There was no time to talk then, none during dinner either. But I knew my friends were bursting with questions. They came after dinner when we had play time.

"What did they want you for?"

"Some people wanted to see me."

"Are they going to adopt you?"

"I think so."

"When?"

"I think in a week."

"Why didn't they take you now?"

"Mrs. McMillan said there was some paperwork she had to do first."

I wished they had taken me now, but I was so enjoying all this attention. Even the matron seemed to look at me differently. She had a little smile like the lady at the reception desk. Yes, Miss Paige must have been in on the secret, too.

The week passed slowly. I was sent to the hospital, where a doctor listened to my chest and thumped my back. He looked in my ears and mouth, made me say "Ah," then gave me a shot.

Finally, the day came. After breakfast I was given all new clothes to put on. Black sateen bloomers, muslin petticoat, blue-and-white-gingham dress, long black stockings, round elastic garters to keep the stockings above my knees, and new black patent leather shoes. I wouldn't have to wear the ones that laced up to my ankles. Finally, I had a red sweater and brown straw hat.

When I was ready to leave, almost everyone gathered around to say good-bye. It was hardest to leave Elsie. She had been my best friend for two years. I would miss her. We hugged and I got a lump in my throat.

A few girls stayed back and looked envious; I didn't blame them. Even Miss Paige looked happy and told me to be a good girl.

Mrs. White came down from her sewing room. She stooped down and gave me a big hug. "Good-bye, dear. I'll think about you when I run elastic in bloomers." She was smiling as she pressed a nickel into my hand, but there were tears in her eyes and that made tears in mine, too.

I never did have a chance to say "good-bye" to Harold. Maybe as a child I was too afraid that if I requested something it might mess up my chances for adoption. Back then they didn't give a child the name of their biological parent or contact information. Nevertheless, it was something I always regretted, for I have always wondered what became of my brother.

"You'd better go now," Miss Paige said and gave me a little pat on the back. So, with waves and good-byes, I trotted off to the main office building.

Mrs. McMillan was waiting for me. "Well, Bernice, this is a big day for us, so we'd best get started. We have a long trip ahead of us."

I walked down the wide stone steps of the orphanage for the last time. Mrs. McMillan opened the car door. The isinglass curtains were snapped down, for it wasn't yet warm enough to travel in an open touring car. I climbed up onto the leather seat as she closed the door and walked around to the other side. Mrs. McMillan was dressed in a dark brown suit with an orange print scarf at the neck. A large brown straw hat sat atop her head with a long hat pin holding it to her thick brown hair. She carried a leather case full of folders and papers. Mrs. McMillan was friendly, and I felt comfortable with her even though there were butterflies in my stomach.

She climbed in on her side and adjusted her long skirt before turning the key. A lever had to be adjusted, then she stepped on a button in the floor. The car shimmied and shuddered, then started with a roar. After pushing the clutch pedal and shifting the long lever, we were on our way.

I looked back at the cluster of buildings that had been my home for two years. *Will I ever see my friends again? And what about Harold?* As we turned a corner, the orphanage disappeared from sight. My nose was pressed nearly against the window as I sat on the edge of my seat.

"When will we get there?"

"Mr. and Mrs. Nesbitt are expecting us for dinner at noon. That will be about three hours."

The new sights filled me with excitement as the long cement highway stretched ahead. I had never seen so many cars. We seemed to meet one every few minutes. Soon farms flew by and occasionally a very small town. Finally, the sound of the motor and the sunshine got the best of me. I fell asleep.

"Wake up, Bernice." Mrs. McMillan was patting me gently on the shoulder. "We're almost there."

FOUR

A
New Home

I sat up and gazed at my surroundings as we rounded a corner onto a gravel road, shifted gears, and ground up a hill. We turned into a driveway that circled around the back of a large stucco house. A big collie dog came barking and wagging his tail. He kept looking back at the house, where Mrs. Nesbitt appeared at the porch screen door.

"Hello," she called. "Be quiet, Jack," she said to the dog.

He stopped barking but kept wagging his tail.

"Come in, come in," said Mrs. Nesbitt. "You've had a long trip, and you must be hungry."

Mrs. McMillan opened the car door for me. I stepped onto the running board, but I wasn't sure about that big dog. I hadn't seen a dog for a long time. He came and smelled my shoes, then looked up, so I cautiously reached down and patted him on the head. It seemed safe, so I stepped down. Now he was close enough to lick my face and we were friends.

Meanwhile, Mrs. Nesbitt and Mrs. McMillan were shaking hands and talking. Mr. Nesbitt appeared at the door and added his greetings. I was feeling uneasy as we all went inside.

The bright kitchen was pale yellow with shiny wood cupboards. The round table in the middle of the room had a new oilcloth set with what I later learned were Blue Willow dishes. The aromas from the big kerosene cookstove were enticing. In the corner stood an ice box with a big round motor on top.

"Bernice, I'll bet you would like to look around the house for a minute. Then you can wash your hands, and we will be ready to eat," Mrs. Nesbitt said as she turned back to the stove.

I walked into the dining room and took in a big breath. I had never seen anything so beautiful. It had pretty flowered wallpaper and a thick Oriental rug with a wide blue border. A large round oak table stood in the middle under a chandelier with five light bulbs that looked like candles. There was a built-in buffet with candlesticks in a holder with long glass prisms hanging all around and a large cut-glass bowl in between. The living room had a rug, too, a fireplace, and comfortable-looking mohair furniture. In the corner sat a beautiful baby grand piano. *I wonder who plays the piano.* The sunroom was open to the living room and had wide windowsills with lots of plants. Windows on each side of the buffet and glass French doors opening onto a big front porch made the room light.

Down the hall I passed another door into the kitchen. Mr. and Mrs. Nesbitt were going over papers with Mrs. McMillan.

Opposite the kitchen door on the other side of the hall was a bedroom. I could see a beautiful oak desk in the corner. Windows all along the side looked into the back yard. Further on I could see a bathroom at the end of the hall and a bedroom on each side. I looked into one. There was a big brass bed, a dresser, and a rocking chair. White ruffled curtains blew gently at an open window. On the bed sat a beautiful doll. *It must really be true then. I will have a room of my own!* I wanted to pick up the doll but decided I'd better not, so I went into the bathroom to wash.

Mrs. Nesbitt appeared in the hall. "Come, dear, we're ready to eat."

Mrs. McMillan and Mr. Nesbitt were already seated at the

table. That seemed strange because at the orphanage we children had always stood behind our chairs. At the sound of a little bell we were supposed to pray a silent prayer. At the second bell we sat down. And when I was really little, at my first home, meal time was not a family occasion. We ate whenever we wanted, wherever we wanted…if there was food.

"Sit down, Bernice," Mrs. McMillan said. So I did, watching to see what would happen next. The collie dog, Jack, sat on the floor between me and Mrs. Nesbitt, watching her every move.

They all bowed their heads and Mr. Nesbitt said, "Oh Lord, we thank thee for this food and all the blessings that we receive. In Jesus' name. Amen."

The food was delicious, even though I hardly knew what I was eating. I never had eaten food like this—and especially not on real china dishes. The adults talked about weather and things I didn't understand, like the economy and politics. I noticed that Mrs. McMillan addressed the Nesbitts as "Ida" and "John."

"Ordinarily, we would not give you a child of this age," Mrs. McMillan was saying. "You are a bit old to be her parents, but we feel this is right for her and for you, too. She never had a stable home situation, but she adjusted quite well in the past and has been obedient. She's a bit behind in school because of a late start and moving, but she seems bright enough. I'm sure you will be good to her."

It suddenly occurred to me that Mrs. McMillan would be leaving and once again I would be left with strangers. They seemed like nice people, but I felt so alone. There had always been other kids around. I couldn't swallow and hard as I tried, I couldn't stop the tears from silently sliding down my cheeks.

"Don't cry, Bernice," Mrs. McMillan said. I hated it when people said "Don't cry." It seemed to make me cry even more.

Mrs. Nesbitt wiped my tears with her napkin, "Bernice, I

think Jack wants a treat," she said cheerily. "Look at what he can do." She broke off a small piece of bread and dropped it above Jack's head. He snapped it up in midair and swallowed it in one gulp. That made me laugh.

"Here, you do it." Mrs. Nesbitt gave me the rest of the slice of bread. I continued dropping bits for Jack to snatch up until it was all gone.

The meal was finished, so Mrs. McMillan got ready to leave. "I'll be back to see you all in a few weeks." She pinned her hat on. "In the meantime, if you have any questions or problems, you can call my office. You have the number."

I noticed the wooden telephone on the wall and wondered what it would be like to talk to someone far away.

"Good-bye, Bernice. Be a good girl, and mind the Nesbitts. They will give you a good home."

After handshakes and good-byes, Mrs. McMillan started the car with a roar. The gravel crunched as the car rolled out of the driveway and down the hill. Then Mrs. McMillan was gone.

I followed Mrs. Nesbitt back into the porch.

"Well, Bernice, I'm sure you have some strange feelings and so do we. We've been wanting a little girl for a long time. If you are happy here, this will always be your home."

"I must be getting back to work," Mr. Nesbitt said. "But after supper you can go to the barn with me while we milk the cows if you like."

After he left, Mrs. Nesbitt started clearing up the dishes.

I wasn't sure what to do. I had never helped in the kitchen, so I just stood there for a minute.

"What shall I call you?" I asked.

"Well, we want you to call us Mama and Daddy. You are our little girl now."

"But I have a Mama."

"I know, dear, but she has said it's all right. She wants you to have a good home."

I didn't quite understand, but it felt better to call them Mother and Dad.

"Since I'm starting a new life I would like to change my name. Everyone says I look a lot like Amelia Earhart, and I admire her very much. I would like to be called Amy now."

"That's a beautiful name. Amy it is, then."

FIVE

Becoming a Farm Kid

"The corn is up, and it looks like a good stand."
Dad stood proudly gazing across the brown field as he had done for many years. His new straw hat was pushed back on his head and his left hand rested lightly on my shoulder.

"I don't see a thing." I stared as hard as I could. "Anyway, what does a 'good stand' mean?"

Dad lowered his tall frame down on one knee to be my height. "See the tracks made by the planter wheels?" He pointed straight ahead. "Exactly between the tracks you can see the little spears. A 'good stand' means almost all the seeds sprouted."

I still couldn't see anything so we walked closer. All of the sudden I could see the rows of tiny shoots only about an inch high. They were curled in little green tubes.

"We'll start cultivating tomorrow. Now, if we have good weather this summer with just enough rain, we'll have good crops." Dad looked farther out. The barley and oat fields were bright green and the alfalfa added another shade of darker green.

"It seems like everything depends on the weather." I was fast learning things that all farm kids knew long before they were my age. The world was filled with wonder.

"How do you know when to plant?" I asked.

"Experience and common sense, I guess. Small grains like oats and barley are planted early. The ground has to be dry enough to work. Corn is planted a little later. There's an old saying: 'When the oak leaves are the size of a squirrel's ear, it's time to plant corn.' If you noticed, the oak trees were the last to leaf out."

For the next few days Dad and the hired man, Walter, cultivated corn. Back and forth across the fields the horses plodded. It wasn't really hard work, but tedious to sit all day looking down at the little green sprouts. The cultivator shovels skimmed just under the surface of the earth to uproot the little weeds and the driver had to keep the horses straight between the rows. The old dog Jack followed until he got tired, then found a shade tree at the end of the field to sleep and wait for Dad.

The noon hour broke the monotony. The men took an hour to eat and rest. The women always had dinner, the biggest meal of the day, ready on time. Walter went to his house and Dad came in through the basement, washed up, and came upstairs to have dinner in the kitchen. We only ate in the dining room on Sundays, holidays, or when we had company.

After dinner Dad rested in his big leather rocking chair for about half an hour, then went back to work promptly at one o'clock.

As a child I was aware that the Nesbitt standard of living was higher than what most people enjoyed in our surrounding communities. Other than overhearing conversations about how others were struggling during these tight times, I grew up almost oblivious to the Depression's impact.

Later in life I learned that Dad had inherited some savings and the farm from his father. He diversified his inheritance into cash, savings, and prudent investments that grew even when the market was crashing.

Further, his fertile Minnesota land produced top yields of hay, grains, and produce. The combination assured that our family was virtually unscathed when the Great Depression wrapped its vicious tentacles in a stranglehold around our nation.

But, looking back, our elevated financial status rarely alienated us from struggling friends and neighbors. Instead the Nesbitt kindness and community involvement secured acceptance and admiration.

Mother and Dad weren't affectionate and didn't give hugs and kisses, but made up for it in other ways. Sometimes I got to ride on the cultivator with Dad. Just being next to him made me feel warm inside. He was gentle and comfortable to be around. I inhaled deeply, taking in the smell of fresh, moist dirt being turned up.

In the evenings I was always around the barn during milking time just watching and learning. It was warm in the barn from the cows. All that could be heard was the quiet munching of the cows eating their grain and Dad humming as he tended to the chores.

"If she's going to be out all the time, she should have overalls," Mother said to Dad. "No use trying to keep her in dresses." So she sent an order to Sears and I got my bib overalls just like Dad's.

Spring was growing warm and I loved running in the fields and being with Dad. He called me "Daddy's little farmhand."

I was beginning to feel like I really did belong here.

Six

Lost in the Woods

It was early summer, and the grass in the pastures was tall enough for good grazing. After the cows were milked in the morning, they were put in the big wood lot for the day. To get there, Dad or Walter drove them down a long fenced path beside the meadow, skirting a wooded area of oak trees. When the gate was closed behind them, the black and white cows were free to leisurely crop grass, drink water from the small lake, and enjoy shade under the oaks on days that became especially hot.

Mother fetched the cows home in the late afternoon in time for evening milking. She would drive our car along the pasture road, open the gate, and make sure the cows started back down the long path toward the barn. Faithful Jack, never missing a chance to ride in the car, accompanied her. Undoubtedly, he also enjoyed being a major part of the cow-moving process. I liked going too.

"I'm going to get the cows a little early this evening," Mother told me at noon. "So you and Jack come about five o'clock to help."

"Why early, Mother?"

"We've invited some friends, the Hendersons, for supper. They live about three farms south of us. I need a little extra time to finish getting supper ready."

About five, I went to the kitchen where Mother had been most of the afternoon.

"M-m-m! It sure smells good in here."

I saw a lemon meringue pie cooling on the table, and Mother was taking a chocolate cake out of the oven.

"James Henderson loves chocolate cake. But it seems to me his wife, Lila, would prefer lemon. Having both means we Nesbitts can have a choice."

"I'm glad I'll have time while we get the cows to think about which I'll choose," I said. "I like them both so much!"

Mother gave me a smile. She loved to cook. I noticed she had said, "we Nesbitts." Even though that was my name now, it still sounded strange. Mother and Daddy never mentioned the fact that recently I had been adopted. That I was not born a Nesbitt. I knew they couldn't have forgotten. Although I was very happy in my new home, it came to my mind every day that I had not always lived here. I was a newcomer. I once had belonged to a different family…a family that didn't keep me.

"What else are we having?"

"I'll fry the pork chops and mash the potatoes as soon as we return with the cows. And lots of homemade applesauce, of course. I made the salad already."

Even though our noon dinners were always big, company meant another grand meal for supper.

At the appointed time, off we went down the pasture road with Jack in the back seat. It hadn't rained for a few days, so billowing clouds of dust rose from behind the car.

Each day, we would find the herd of about thirty black and

white heifers waiting near the gate, looking down the road, chewing, chewing, chewing.

"It seems cows are always chewing. What are they chewing on?" I asked Mother.

"Their cud."

"What's a cud?"

"Well, you see, cows have four stomachs," Mother explained. "What they eat all goes into the first stomach. Then when they rest they kind of burp up a mouthful at a time and chew it again."

"Oh, ick." I made a face.

The cows were eager to get home at milking time because their full bags were uncomfortable, sometimes even dripping a little. Also, they probably looked forward to the ration of grain they would get in the barn. But today, because we were early, the cows were nowhere in sight.

"Oh dear," said Mother. "I didn't plan on them not being here yet."

Cows or no cows, I jumped out to open the gate while mother turned the car around. Ordinarily at this point Jack would begin circling the mooing animals to get them moving toward home.

Returning to the car, I asked, "Where are they?"

"It's a hot day. They must be in the woods."

"How do they know it's early? How do they tell time?"

"They just seem to know. Probably their full bags of milk tell them. Maybe they see the shadows."

"If they're in the woods, I can find them," I said confidently. Mother agreed to let me search. With Jack at my side, I headed across the meadow in the direction of the stand of great oaks.

I had been in the woods once before, but not alone. Together, Jack and I could get the job done. Following a well-worn cows' path we climbed up a slope. At the top of the rise I glanced back. Mother was standing at the gate. I waved and she waved back. I went down the back side of the slope into the trees, my collie friend running ahead. When I glanced back again, Mother was out of sight.

It was much darker in the woods. Gnarled oaks and great spreading elms hid the sky and cast eerie shadows. Low bramble bushes closed in the lower spaces. Except for birds twittering overhead, it was quiet. Then a sudden noise close to me made my heart race. Only a squirrel! Jack stopped to look at me, his tongue hanging out one side of his mouth. He seemed to be laughing as he stood wagging his tail. With heart still pounding, I continued to walk farther, following the narrow path and avoiding thorny brambles as best I could. Suddenly, the path branched off in two other directions. Which way should I go? I couldn't decide.

"Jack! We're lost!"

Jack stood looking at me as if for directions. I turned down what looked to be the most worn path. Everything around me seemed threatening.

Will Mother wait for me?

The thought was terrifying.

My mama abandoned me in scary places when I was little—like the time I woke up in a saloon and she was gone....

It'll be nighttime soon. What wild animals are in these woods? Wolves maybe?

Even though the early evening air was cool among the trees, I was getting very warm.

I've been gone such a long time!

Suddenly I glimpsed a patch of bright sunshine ahead. As I headed toward it, Jack slipped around me, running ahead.

"No! Don't leave me, Jack," I pleaded. But he paid no attention.

In the clearing the cows were contentedly cropping grass. They lifted their heads to look up at us with their big, round eyes. What a relief! I wondered if they were surprised to see us. *Now to drive them around the woods and toward home.*

Jack barked and circled around. Immediately all the cows started moving in the same direction. But it was the wrong way! They were heading for the woods! I waved my arms, trying to head them off, but they ignored me. We were in the trees again, and it was darker than ever. Brambles caught at my clothes, trying to trap me. Jack stayed alongside the cows, not helping at all to move them back to the pasture. Tears mixed with sweat on my dusty, hot face. Mosquitoes and gnats bit my arms as I tried to shoo them away. I pulled my hair free when it became caught in low branches. The trees all looked the same. Every path looked the same. How would I ever get the cows to go the right way? Finally, there was nothing to do but stumble along, hardly seeing through my tears, and follow the herd.

Is Mother looking for me? Is she worried? Will she be upset with me because she's late making supper for the company?

To my amazement, there was the meadow and way over there was Mother still standing at the gate! Jack was loping around the cows with an air of importance. He herded them along the path that traversed the grassy, sun-drenched rise.

I wiped my grimy face on my sleeve and grinned as I hurried toward Mother. The cows were moving into their familiar lane with Jack at their feet.

"Well, Amy, that didn't take you long at all," Mother praised. "You and Jack did a good job."

I never told her how scared I had been, or how glad I was that the cows and Jack brought *me* home.

We had a pleasant meal with the Hendersons. As the grown-ups talked, I thought about my scary adventure in the woods, and how happy I was to see Mother waiting for me. I didn't need to fear being lost any more. I felt more safe than ever before.

After supper, I helped Mother clear away the plates before she served dessert. When we were by the sink, I asked in a whisper if I could have lemon pie *and* chocolate cake. It was sort of a private celebration.

Seven

The State Fair

One August evening, Dad looked up from the newspaper he was reading and announced he'd like to go to the State Fair in the morning.

Mother was enthusiastic. "Oh, good! Amy, you'll like the fair. You can help me find handmade crafts for Christmas gifts. And we can watch the home-making demonstrations. They always give me new ideas."

"I see in the paper there will be some fine animals to look over tomorrow." Dad looked over at me with a twinkle in his eye. "I suppose this year we'll have to stop by the Midway rides. I haven't ridden a Ferris wheel in a long while. Do you think they still sell cotton candy?"

Ferris wheel? Cotton candy? What in the world were they talking about? I felt myself getting excited too. I had never known adults who would take a day off to have a good time. The Minnesota State Fair was another first in my life, as so much was since I came to live with the Nesbitts. I had a new home, new parents, and even a new name. Everything seemed like an adventure since I had been adopted. I could hardly sleep that night.

My first impression of the fairgrounds was hundreds of people, some pushing and shoving, all laughing and talking in the merry atmosphere. Barkers shouted for attention; happy music swirled from several directions. I held tight to Dad's hand as we walked, breathing in the aroma of popcorn. I soon figured out what cotton candy was as children passed us holding big, beautiful, pink fluff on a stick. We saw bumper cars, a roller coaster, and an arcade where people threw darts at balloons to win stuffed animals. Everything looked fun, but what caught my eye was the enormous Ferris wheel.

"Oh!...can I go on a ride?" I asked, jumping up and down.

"Mother would like to look at things in the pavilion first, and I want to walk through the animal barns," said Dad. "You'll enjoy seeing how many different kinds of chickens and sheep there are. Then we'll come back to ride the Ferris wheel."

Everywhere I looked there was so much to see I couldn't take it all in. In one long building we admired countless displays of cakes, pies, and cookies. Dad explained that judges had tasted every entry and awarded prizes for the best.

"I'd sure like that job," I told Mother.

We took special notice of the baked goods with blue and red ribbons. Blue was first place, and red was second. Mother took time to quickly jot down a couple recipes she'd like to try. Then we walked through the sewing and knitting displays. Mother was teaching me to knit, so I was interested in the intricate cables and other patterns. So far I had learned only two stitches—knit and purl.

I was amazed to see some very fancy lace.

"It's called tatting," Mother explained. "It's done with a

shuttle and thread." Mother knew so many things.

The quilts were especially beautiful. My favorite was a pattern called "Log Cabin." We had a few quilts at home that Mother's sister had made. One was called "Starburst."

If our quilts were entered in the fair, I bet they'd win first place.

After looking through the home and garden building, Dad suggested it was time for all of us to go to the animal barns. They, of course, were what interested him most.

I didn't know there were so many kinds of chickens. My favorite was the Banties with their long red tail feathers. And the rabbits! There were adorable whites with pink noses and cute floppy-eared browns. I was able to pet a few and offer them some crunchy carrots.

Then Dad steered us over to the horses and cattle. Again, I got an education, this time about varieties of cows. I had thought all cows were black and white like ours, but Dad showed me brown Herefords and Black Angus. I was a little timid around any cattle with long horns. They looked dangerous. When Dad had seen everything, I wasn't sorry to leave the barns, because they were hot and smelly.

About one o'clock, we were lured by the smell of hotdogs and ate them, with lots of mustard and chopped pickles, at a picnic table.

Mother noticed me eying the children at the next table eating cotton candy.

"Amy, why don't you take this nickel and go over to the clown over there with the big red nose and funny shoes, and buy some cotton candy for yourself."

Mother and Dad smiled as they watched me dissolve the sweet confection on my tongue. It wasn't long before I was a sticky mess. Mother took me to the restroom and used her hankie to clean me up.

On the way back to meet Dad, I was startled to spot the

back of a boy who looked just like my brother Harold. I left Mother's side to run after him.

"Amy! Come back." I heard Mother, but I couldn't respond. This was too important. I had not seen Harold for so long.

"Harold!" I shouted. "Harold!"

Not hearing me, the boy turned a corner. For a moment I lost him in the crowd, but then caught sight of him again.

"Harold," I screamed and ran faster. Finally, I caught up with the boy and grabbed his coat.

"Hey!" he said turning around.

My heart sank as I looked into a face I didn't recognize. "I'm sorry," I managed to say. "I thought you were...someone else."

From that day on, whenever I was in a big crowd, I searched for the faces of my birth mother and Harold. Of course, it wasn't reasonable to think I'd see them at the State Fair. My family was too poor to even buy a ticket to get in the gate. We had never gone on a picnic or to a fair. And, as far as I knew, Harold was still in the orphanage. No one at the orphanage ever got to go to the Minnesota State Fair, or much of any place.

Trembling, and with tears streaming down my face, I watched the boy disappear into a building. I began to cry uncontrollably. I felt like I was choking.

Both Dad and Mother caught up with me. Dad got down on his knees and wrapped his arms around me. He was out of breath. "Amy, what's the matter? What happened?"

"I thought I saw my brother." I sobbed into his shoulder.

"Oh! Amy...I'm so sorry." He continued to hold me as I struggled to compose myself.

Seeing Harold—and then it wasn't Harold—made me feel anger and grief that could not be contained. I couldn't seem to stop crying.

"We were so worried. Please don't ever run off like that

again." Mother's hands were on my shoulders. I glanced up at her and thought her eyes looked a little wet. We were in the middle of a busy street with chattering people all around us.

After a moment, Dad said, "Amy, I think I see a carousel over there. Would you like to ride a pretty horse?" He wiped my tears with his handkerchief.

I nodded.

Nothing more was said about my brother or my running off.

"Dad and I will be right here by the rail watching you as you go 'round and 'round," Mother assured me.

The man who operated the carousel helped me climb up onto a creamy white horse with pink reins and pastel flowers around its neck. I felt like a princess in a fairy tale and was able to smile again. As the music started, the carousel began to move forward and my horse gently rose and fell, up and down, on its pole. I waved at Mother and Dad each time I passed.

Next, Dad said he'd like to ride on the Ferris wheel with me. Our seat swung gently back and forth as we rose higher and higher. At the top we could see the whole fairgrounds covered with tiny people and roofs. I had never been up so high, but I wasn't afraid with Dad sitting next to me.

We didn't leave the fairgrounds until the sun went down. It had been a full day, and all three of us were tired. We were hardly out of the parking lot before I fell asleep in the back seat.

Eight

Preparing for the Holidays

When summer became fall, Mother took me to Bloomington Elementary School and registered me for the third grade. I liked it better than the orphanage school. Our teacher was just as strict as Mrs. Conoway, but we also had more fun. My reading ability improved so much that I really enjoyed the stories in my third-grade reader.

The Friday after Thanksgiving there was no school.

"We'll go shopping tomorrow," Mother said. "We need to get everything to make fruitcake."

"What's fruitcake?" I asked.

"Well, it's a cake we only have at Christmastime that's full of raisins, nuts, cherries, and citron."

"Why only at Christmas time?"

"Because that makes it special. If we had it at other times it wouldn't be special."

Swenson's was a little general store near us, but they didn't have the things Mother wanted. Neither did Hill's Mercantile. We went all the way to Minneapolis to go shopping. There she bought seeded raisins, seedless raisins, white raisins, dried currants, maraschino cherries, dried figs, dried dates, citron, and walnuts. Then, of course, there were all the everyday things we needed.

Mother always gave me a nickel to spend when we went to the store. All the while she was making her selections, I stood in front of the glass candy counter trying to decide what I would buy. How difficult! Finally, when Mother was finished, the grocer came behind the counter.

"Well, little lady, have you made up your mind?"

"I think so. I'll have two root beer barrels, two licorice whips, and a penny's worth of cinnamon drops." There was a little glass measuring scoop in the bin for that. One scoop was one penny's worth. Sometimes, if it was at the bottom of the bin he would give me the little glass scoop. "Oh, and four lemon drops and one gum drop."

The man put my candies in a little bag and handed it to me. "A very nice selection," he said and gave Mother a little wink. She smiled back at him.

It was a good feeling to go home with all these good things to eat. I breathed in the mingled aromas of fresh ground coffee, big juicy oranges, and the wonderful fruitcake spices. When I was little, there had rarely been enough to eat. This great quantity of food made me feel guilty when I thought of my brother, Harold, and the kids at the orphanage. The adults were always talking about the Great Depression. They said people were without jobs and couldn't feed their families, yet we had such abundance. I heard Mother and Dad say several times that we were fortunate to be so comfortable in these times.

Every day brought me new adventures and new things to learn. It seemed that giving me new experiences was Mother and Dad's way of showing love. Since the weather was colder and I was spending more time indoors, Mother began teaching me to cook. I had loved being Dad's little shadow in the fields and barn during the spring and summer, and now I found it was also fun to help Mother in the kitchen.

On Saturday morning Mother said, "You can chop up figs, dates, nuts, and cherries. Then put everything into a large bowl and mix them." She put a little flour into the mixture so the fruits wouldn't stick together.

It took me quite awhile, but I felt important chopping with the big sharp knife. Mother checked my work and said I had done a good job.

"I'll cream the sugar, butter, and eggs. Then you can help stir in the flour, milk, spices, and baking powder. We will mix in the fruits and nuts last."

I had a little footstool to stand on so I'd be tall enough to help make the fruitcake. The dough filled four loaf pans and baked for a long time.

Ummmm, it smelled wonderful. Finally, they came out of the oven.

"Can I taste it now?"

"Oh, no. It's not ready yet."

"Why not?" I asked, inhaling the rich aroma deeply. "I thought everything came out of the oven ready to eat."

Mother tipped the loaves on their sides. "The fruitcake must cool. Then we'll wrap each loaf in cloths with a little brandy on them. After that we'll put each one into the big crock downstairs until Christmas."

Christmas! I was disappointed. A whole month was a long time to wait to taste this wonderful-smelling treat.

What a busy time Christmas was. Mother spent many hours writing Christmas cards, adding a note or letter to most of them. I joined my classmates selling Christmas seals for the Tuberculosis Association. December school activities centered on Christmas. I loved learning Christmas carols and listening to the Christmas stories our teacher read. One of the special things about my new school was that I had crayons of my own to use during our art projects. When I took my creations home, Mother and Daddy always admired them. Mother said I could add my long red and green paper chain to our beautiful Christmas tree. Dad said it was just the right touch.

Every Sunday Mother, Dad, and I attended a small country church about two miles from our home. Mother was the head of the children's Sunday school. I learned it was a tradition to have a Christmas Eve program, and that the 25 or 30 children would all have a piece to memorize and recite that evening.

"There'll also be a Christmas tree and gifts at the church," Mother said.

"Will everyone get something?" I remembered how at the orphanage each child received one small gift, like jacks or a jump rope.

"Yes, of course, and you can help me wrap them."

Mother brought out a box filled with new long black stockings and some Christmas wrapping paper. Using a list of names, together we decided what size for each girl and wrapped and tagged each pair. Then we did the same with shorter, thicker socks for the boys.

I had discovered the Sears Roebuck catalog last summer when Mother had ordered my overalls. What a magical book! I poured over its pages, especially the toy section. I hadn't known so many wonderful things to play with even existed.

"What would you like for Christmas, Amy?" Mother asked one evening as she watched me thumb through the catalog.

I didn't know what to say. I had never been asked that

question before. The day I arrived a new doll was on my bed. Mother was teaching me to sew by making doll clothes. On the Fourth of July I got a puppy. My parents already had given me so much that I really didn't need anything, nor did I feel worthy of more.

"Maybe a good book," was all I could think of. Mother enjoyed reading and often brought books home from the library for me. I liked to read to myself, but it was even better when she read to me. She promised that once Christmas was over we would start reading *Little Women* together.

We were busy for the next several weeks preparing for Christmas. It seemed like Mother kept saying, "When you get through with that, Amy, I'll show you what to do next."

One December Saturday, Mother and I drove to Minneapolis for a day of shopping. Early in the morning before we left home, Dad checked our 1930 Packard for gas and tested the air in the tires. "I want you to have a safe trip," he said.

Always "the lady," mother never went anywhere without her hat and gloves. On this day, she wore her best brown wool coat with its fur collar, tan kid gloves, and a tan felt hat. I wore a dress and my church coat, and my best shoes.

The big city had a dusting of light snow. Looking down each street I could see evergreen garlands and big red balls hanging from street lamps. From the street, we drove into Dayton's department store garage, where a uniformed man handed Mother a ticket. I had been to Dayton's twice before—first in May, when I had come to live at the Nesbitts with nothing but what I was wearing, and later in the fall to buy school clothes.

This time, when we entered the store, we stepped into a holiday wonderland. I caught my breath trying to take in the twinkling lights and glittery colors of each display. Even the ceiling was festooned with decorations. I had a hard time looking around and keeping track of Mother at the same time. She watched me with a smile. I think it gave her pleasure to see things once again through my eyes.

We bought many things that day. I was fitted with new school shoes because mine were getting too small. Then we selected some blue wool fabric and a pattern for a dress for me. After that, there were gifts to select for relatives. Each time Mother paid for something, she wrote on a slip of paper and handed it to the clerk. I was learning about writing checks, something I had never heard of. The sales girls copied a number from our garage ticket in order to store our purchases until we were finished shopping. It didn't feel right to me to walk away empty-handed; I thought it looked special to walk around the store carrying packages. But Mother said this way was best.

Mother was a careful shopper. She spent a lot of time examining things before making a purchase. As she considered what to buy, I took my time admiring beautifully beaded handbags and sparkling jeweled necklaces in their glass cases.

"Let's have lunch before the tea room gets too crowded," Mother said as she guided me toward the elevators. Uniformed women wearing funny pill box hats announced each floor as they opened and closed the glass doors with their brass trim.

"Fourth floor: dining room to your left."

Eating in the dining room was very elegant. From the windows we could see far into the distance. Mother pointed out the dome of the state capitol.

"St. Paul and Minneapolis are called the Twin Cities because they are side by side."

"Can we see our farm from here?" I asked, craning my neck.

"No, I think it's too far. It would be over there where you see rolling hills." Mother pointed to the west.

What I really was looking for was my old orphanage; but, of course, I had no idea where to look. Being even this close to Harold made me look down onto the street below and wonder if he ever walked there. I hoped he was warm enough.

Mother thought eating in a nice restaurant was a good experience for me. She said I needed to learn good manners so I would be comfortable in any situation where nice manners were expected. When Mother said, "act like a lady," I knew good manners were needed.

Suddenly, one pea dropped off my fork and rolled all the way down my dress leaving a buttery trail.

"Oh, dear. Now we'll have to get your dress dry cleaned," she said.

Even though I always tried so hard to please, it seemed I often embarrassed Mother, like spilling a glass of water once when we had company, and another time my meat landed on the tablecloth when I was trying to cut it. There were lots of rules. I learned when there was more than one fork to start from the outside and work in. And I should wipe the bottom of my spoon on the edge of the bowl away from me when I ate soup. Bread was to be broken in half before buttering it.

There was a picture on the bottom of each child's plate or bowl depicting a children's story. I looked forward to eating all my meal because it was fun to see what picture I would find at the bottom. Often she had to remind me to slow down.

In midafternoon, when we finished our shopping, we returned to the parking garage. Mother handed the valet her ticket. He brought the car to us and loaded all our purchases into the back seat. Mother turned on the heater against the winter chill, and it wasn't long before I was asleep. It had been a happy but exhausting day. I could hardly wait for my first Christmas as a Nesbitt.

NINE

Christmas

Finally, it was Christmas Eve. I knew my part perfectly for the evening program at church. The afternoon's rehearsal was the last of two, and it went well, even though everyone was flushed with nervous excitement. Mrs. Swenson, whom I had met several times at Swenson's General Store, directed the program. She was pleased we knew our memorized pieces so well. Even though my lines were fairly simple, I had been saying them over and over in my head for days. Those who were going to wear simple costumes tried them on and walked to their places at the front of the church. Mrs. Swenson assured us she would be seated close-by tonight to prompt us if necessary.

Several people remained after the rehearsal to decorate the plump fir tree that stood to one side at the front of the sanctuary. Under Mother's direction, I got to attach evergreen boughs with red ribbons to the altar rail.

Once back home, we ate an early supper of leftovers, "to make room in the ice box for tomorrow," Mother said.

Mother made a new Christmas dress for me of the navy blue wool from Dayton's. It was trimmed with rows of little red French knots around the collar and cuffs and tiny rosebud buttons down the front. I told her it was the most beautiful dress I had ever owned or even seen.

"Walter and I plan to do the milking early," Dad said. "In

fact, he's already started. We need to leave for church about 7 o'clock." Walter's wife, Evie, had a baby last March. The three of them lived in the old farmhouse on the other side of the barnyard. This would be little Freddie's first Christmas.

I had just enough time to bathe before dressing for church. While I was in the tub, I thought about Christmas Eves back at the orphanage. *What are Elsie and the other girls doing right now? Is Harold okay? I wonder if he misses me....*

I recalled last year how Miss Paige had summoned us girls from the basement playroom to the living room. Christmas was one of the few times we were allowed to be in that special place. We giggled all the way up the stairs. A good-sized tree had been set up in the tower corner. It was decorated with strings of popcorn and cranberries. All eyes went eagerly to the wrapped packages underneath. Miss Paige tried to lead us in a few Christmas carols, but we were more interested in gazing at the gifts, lights, and tinsel. Finally, the matrons distributed the presents at random, one to each girl. Inside, we found a jump rope, ball, picture book, jacks, or a soft doll (nothing with small parts that would get lost). It was understood by all that the gifts were community property, not for exclusive enjoyment.

A few girls received packages from relatives. I waited expectantly, but there wasn't one for me. Leaving piles of crumpled gift wrap and ribbon on the carpet, we clamored downstairs to play with the new toys.

"Amy, are you still in the bathtub?" Mother's voice coming through the door brought me back to the present.

"Yes, Mother."

"You'd better hurry. Dad will want to shave, and I'd like to use the bathroom, too."

"Okay. I'll be right out."

I quickly dried myself while the tub was draining, and dashed into my room, where Mother had laid out my clothes. My clean long underwear, warming on the radiator, went on first. Then long white cotton stockings attached to garters with safety pins, followed by white sateen bloomers, a petticoat, black patent leather shoes, and finally the beautiful new dress. I was ready.

I couldn't resist going into the living room for one more look. The softly glowing tree lights were the only illumination. A gorgeous angel with white feather wings and a gold crown stood majestically at the top. This angel worried me a bit, because at school each student in my class had laboriously glued hundreds of tiny glass beads onto a silver cardboard star as a tree topper gift for our parents. This was my only gift for Mother and Dad. How could it compare to this heavenly creature that now floated so gracefully?

Neat stacks of packages under the tree waited for relatives who would come tomorrow for Christmas dinner. Many other gifts, in all shapes and sizes, had my name on them.

In the dining room, Mother had added leaves to the table extending it as far as it would go, and it was already set with her best china and silver. The buffet mirror, the candlestick prisms in front of it, and the crystal goblets on the table caught the tree lights, reflecting magical bursts of color. Logs in the fireplace were ready to be lit, and from the mantle hung a red stocking with holly leaves and the name *Amy* embroidered on it.

I couldn't remember ever before hanging up a stocking for Santa. Of course, I didn't really believe in Santa Claus, because he had never come to the orphanage. If he were real, wouldn't it be there, of all places, he would go? But I wanted to please Mother and Dad, so I went along with their pretending.

"It's time to leave, Amy. Put on your coat and hat. Dad's gone out to warm up the car."

Mother was wearing her good brown coat with the fur collar and matching hat. She pulled on brown, fur-lined gloves.

"Do I have to wear overshoes?" I hated to cover my pretty patent leather shoes.

"Yes. I think you'd better. Hard telling where we'll have to park and you don't want to get your new shoes muddy." Warmer temperatures today had made most of the snow melt. I hoped for a new snowfall overnight.

The little crowded church was brightly lit that lovely Christmas Eve. Friends and neighbors seemed to greet each other with extra warmth. The tree, festooned with decorations, stood in glittering splendor in its corner, while a small choir wearing burgundy robes sat on the other side. The curved altar railing with "my" greenery formed a small stage. I was quietly pleased that I was able to contribute in small ways to the evening's festive atmosphere.

The program began. Mary, cradling a baby doll wrapped in a white blanket, Joseph holding a lamp, bath-robed shepherds, and winged angels made their entrance from the side sanctuary door, taking their places on the little stage. They recited verses from the Bible, telling the nativity story. The last shepherd's speaking part was the cue for me to walk up onto the stage with two of my school classmates. We placed ourselves strategically around the central players. Clarence began reciting his lines which were the first verse of the song, "Away in a Manger."

> *Away in a manger, no crib for a bed,*
> *The little Lord Jesus laid down His sweet head.*
> *The stars in the sky looked down where He lay,*
> *The Little Lord Jesus, asleep on the hay.*

I had asked Mother what a manger was. She told me it was like the feeding troughs that were in the barn where Dad put hay for the cows during milking. That was a surprise. It meant little baby Jesus had been born in a barn! I wondered if it smelled like ours. Was it very cold?

Then Rosemary, another girl in my class, recited the second verse.

> *The cattle are lowing, the baby awakes,*
> *But little Lord Jesus, no crying He makes.*
> *I love Thee, Lord Jesus, look down from the sky,*
> *And stay by my cradle 'til morning is nigh.*

I wondered how the baby kept from crying? *Does Jesus look down at me at night while I am sleeping?* It was finally my turn to speak the third verse I had practiced for so long.

> *Be near me, Lord Jesus, I ask Thee to stay*
> *Close by me forever, and love me, I pray.*
> *Bless all the dear children in Thy tender care,*
> *And take us to heaven to live with Thee there.*

What a relief! I had not forgotten a word. I looked into the crowd and saw Mother and Dad both smiling broadly at me, but oddly, with tears streaming down their cheeks.

Mrs. Swenson went to the piano and began to play the music to the words we had just spoken. We all sang, and she gestured the congregation to join us. At the end, we children filed off stage and sat down in the front chairs that had been reserved for us.

Mrs. Swenson continued playing several carols and the congregation stood and sang joyfully. This year I knew and loved these Christmas carols, thanks to our music teacher at school. My favorite of all was "O Holy Night." As we sang the beautiful words, I wondered about their meaning.

O holy night! The stars are brightly shining,
It is the night of the dear Savior's birth;
Long lay the world in sin and error pining,
Till He appeared and the soul felt its worth.
A thrill of hope the weary world rejoices,
For yonder breaks a new and glorious morn.

Fall on your knees
Oh, hear the angel voices!
O night divine
O night when Christ was born!

When we sang, "O night divine!" I felt a happy thrill go through me. *Divine. That's what Christmas is. Divine.*

When the singing was finished, the minister said a prayer and gave a benediction.

Suddenly, a loud "Ho, Ho, Ho" was heard from the back of the church. Santa burst in, wearing a rumpled red costume and tattered beard. Tiny tots clung to their mothers, older children were amused, and teenagers scoffed a bit, but all willingly accepted the little bags of candy Santa distributed. I quickly peeked into my bag, happy to see several pieces of my favorite striped ribbon candy.

Then, amidst much commotion, Mother signaled that it was time to distribute the gifts we had prepared a few weeks earlier. She and I, with a couple of helpers, matched name tags to children, so each one received the right size and kind of stockings. In addition, there was a package for me containing a necklace and several handkerchiefs.

With the gifts distributed, blessings of "Merry Christmas" were heard as families began to gather their belongings and head out into the cold night air to their cars.

Back at home, Mother looked over the dining table to make sure everything was ready for tomorrow, while I lingered by the tree, again wondering about the star I had made. On the kitchen counter was a big wicker basket filled with fruit, sweets, and soft baby toys. A bright green ribbon cascaded from the handle. Mother had prepared this as a Christmas gift basket for Walter, Evie, and little Freddie.

"Off to bed now, Amy. Tomorrow will be a big day." A few minutes later, she came into my room to tuck me in. It felt good to snuggle under my down quilt.

The next thing I knew, the basement door banged. It was morning! Dad was already back from milking. I jumped out of bed and dashed down the hall in my pajamas. The smell of coffee and bacon frying mingled with the fragrance of evergreen.

"Can we open presents now? Can we?" I jumped around like a monkey.

"We may as well. There'll be no peace 'til we do." Mother laughed as she removed her apron.

Dad came, smiling, up the basement stairs and asked what in the world all the commotion was. He told us how pleased Walter was when Dad gave him the gift basket this morning. "You should have seen his face when he saw those big oranges and the apples and candies. You'd have thought he was a young boy. And, Ida, he told me to thank you kindly for the toys you made for the baby." Mother looked pleased. "They'll be driving to St. Paul as soon as they can leave to spend the day with Evie's mother."

Finally, Dad turned to me with a twinkle in his eye. "What do you suppose Santa brought you?" he teased.

"Oh, Dad." This was not the time to say I didn't believe in Santa.

Laughing, I dragged him by the hand while he pretended to hold back. In the living room, I gasped. In addition to the many packages I had memorized yesterday, there were now, without wrappings, a new sled, a shiny red wagon, a mechanical train, and a round box filled with Tinker Toys. It looked as if we had entered a wonderful toy store.

"How did all these things get here? Where did you hide them?"

Mother and Dad winked and smiled at each other. They enjoyed surprises as much as I did.

I stood in the middle of the room overwhelmed, not knowing quite what to do in the midst of such bounty. Mother suggested I start with my Christmas stocking, so I lifted the bulging sock from its hook on the mantle and spilled its contents onto the sofa. It held numerous small toys, puzzles, nuts, candy, and an orange in the toe.

"Thank you, Santa Claus!" I said, purposely to no one in particular.

Dad laughed out loud.

Feeling more comfortable, I got down on my hands and knees by the tree and scooted back and forth, selecting a first present. Then, happily settling into the task at hand, I tore into one gift after another, each labeled with my name.

New clothes, dolls, books, and a beautiful white rabbit fur coat with a matching hat were just some of the abundance I received. After opening each present, I was careful to say an enthusiastic, "Thank you!" But that hardly seemed adequate. By the end, I sank with happy weariness against the sofa while Mother and Dad exchanged their own gifts. There was a string of pearls for Mother, and a leather desk set for Dad.

Then I remembered the star. I pulled it out from behind the pile of gifts for the relatives and handed it to Mother. "This is something I made for you and Dad at school," I said. "It isn't very much."

Mother removed the tissue paper wrapping. "Oh, Amy! It's lovely! This must have been a lot of work. Look, John; it's an ornament for the top of the tree. Can you put it up?"

"Well, well," Dad said. "Very pretty, Amy."

He reached up high with his long arms and carefully tipped the top branch toward him so he could remove the feathery angel and hand it to Mother. She placed it on the buffet between the prism candlestick holders. The star was pasted to a green cardboard cone. Dad put the cone over the branch where the angel had been. The star nodded forward a bit because it was heavier than the angel had been. Even though the early morning sunshine was only weakly coming through the windows, the glass beads caught some rays and flashed the glitter I had hoped.

Mother gave me an appreciative look. "Thank you, Amy. There has never been a nicer ornament."

She stooped to gather some of the torn wrappings and ribbons. "And now we'd better have breakfast. We've got lots to do before everyone arrives."

"I'll need to finish cleaning the barn and then clear the driveway. I'm glad it was only a light snow last night." Dad sat down at the kitchen table while Mother poured his coffee. "Uncle Willard, Marion, and little Audrey will be coming all the way from Excelsior in their Model T and wouldn't appreciate getting stuck when they get here."

"Who else is coming?" I asked. I had met almost all my

new relatives but didn't know them well because most of them lived about twenty miles away.

"Well, Ethyl and Bill will bring their two little girls, Mary and Barbara. And, of course, Uncle Knute and Aunt Annie and Burton will be here." Mother peeked into the oven, where the stuffing in the huge turkey was beginning to waft a wonderful aroma of sage, onions, and celery.

Aunt Annie was Dad's sister who lived on the farm next to ours. Cousin Burton was eleven, about two years older than I. Of the children coming I knew him the best, because we had played together on several occasions. Little Cousin Audrey appeared to be almost three. Mary and Barbara, ages four and seven, were not cousins, but friends who lived close by.

After breakfast, the morning flew by because I was so busy with my new toys. Mother occasionally called me to give her a hand. "Amy, please go downstairs and fill this pan to the top with potatoes, and then bring the cranberries in from the porch."

I ran my fingers through the round, bright red fruit. Curious, I bit into one. "Ugh! It's sour!" I said, spitting it out.

"Well, they're not very good raw." Mother was always amused when I discovered something new. "I'm sure you'll like them better when they're cooked with sugar to make a sauce."

About noon, relatives began arriving bearing pies and more packages. I was introduced to Aunt Susan, who came with candy and brightly wrapped gifts. A smiley, roundish woman, she wasn't really an aunt, but a friend of Mother's who worked as a nurse.

Red-faced from the cold, our cheerful guests shook hands

and quickly took off coats and overshoes. Thick lap robes were brought in from the cars and draped over heat radiators to warm them for the trip home. The house was bustling with activity and conversation. We girls showed off our new dolls to each other. Of course, Burton was more interested in my train set and Tinker Toys. What fun we all had.

The ladies helped with last-minute preparations, then began scurrying back and forth from kitchen to dining room carrying in brimming bowls of food until the table was practically covered. When the potatoes were mashed and the gravy bubbling hot, Mother entered with the golden brown turkey ringed with green parsley and red crabapples, placing its platter at the head of the table. We three Nesbitts and our many guests gathered around and Dad said grace. Then we all sat except Dad, who stood to carve the turkey with a great flourish.

"White meat or dark?" he asked each guest. There was joking and chattering while plates were filled to heaping with mashed potatoes, gravy, stuffing, squash, creamed peas, carrots, various salads, homemade rolls and, of course, the beautifully red cranberry sauce, now much sweeter.

This was one of those "good manners" times that Mother had trained me for. I was to "act like a lady." At a gathering with guests, children were to speak only when spoken to and be on their best behavior, especially at the table. If I tipped over my milk, or spilled food on my dress, horrors! Mother would be very embarrassed. So I was a little nervous but managed to eat my share of the great feast without making any observable mistakes.

Finally, it was dessert time. The ladies rose to help serve this last course. Mother's specialty was called plum pudding, even though it didn't seem to have any plums in it. I had watched her make it with ground suet, flour, spices, molasses, walnuts, raisins, and milk. She steamed it for several hours in jars set in boiling water. Now Mother spooned the pudding into dishes and topped it with a hot, sweet, buttery white sauce.

In addition, several pies and a variety of Christmas cookies were placed on the table, alongside slices of the rich fruitcake that had been resting in the crock in the basement since the day after Thanksgiving. After weeks of anticipation, I finally was able to taste this treat, remembering how I had helped to make it.

At last we could eat no more. I wondered if everyone's stomach was feeling as stretched as mine. Mother excused us children to play because we were getting restless, but the adults remained at the table, talking and sipping coffee. Mary, Barbara, and I were happy to get back to our doll family on the rug in front of the fireplace, while Burton continued to assemble train tracks. Little Audrey happily tossed around some Christmas ribbons until she got fussy and Aunt Marion put her on Mother and Dad's bed for a nap.

Eventually, everyone left the table. The men retired to the living room, and the ladies stored the leftover food and washed the dishes.

As Mother and Aunt Susan walked back and forth putting the china away in the dining room buffet, Mother inquired how things were at Green Lake Sanitarium where Aunt Susan was the superintendent of nurses. When Mother was younger, they had worked together at a tubercular sanitarium in Pennsylvania.

"I'll be retiring soon. Maybe in a couple of years," Aunt Susan said. "Then I'm thinking of doing some volunteer missionary work in the Ozarks."

"Oh, that's wonderful," Mother said. "I've heard there are great needs in that part of the country."

Aunt Susan and Mother were as close as sisters. When I first arrived at the Nesbitts, she had brought me a beautiful doll. She had made all the clothes for it herself—dress, petticoat, bloomers, a blue wool cape and cap. Once when Mother and I had visited, Aunt Susan had showed me her collection of antique dolls and all the clothes she had made for them.

When the dishes were finished, everyone sat in the living room to exchange gifts. The craft items Mother had purchased last fall at the State Fair were kindly received. Aunt Marion had crocheted a lace doily for each woman. Ethel made fudge and peanut brittle for all. Aunt Susan gave Dad a knitted scarf. The children each received a small toy.

It seemed only a short time until Dad went to change his clothes for evening chores. Uncle Knute and Burton went home to do their milking as well. Bill borrowed some of Dad's work clothes and went out to help Dad, since Walter had been given Christmas Day off. He was shorter than Dad, so he looked kind of funny with the overall legs rolled up. I couldn't help but realize what a big responsibility it was to raise animals. Cows needed milking, even on Christmas Day. When the work was done, all the men came back because it was time to eat again.

The ladies brought out the leftovers that so recently had been put away. Everyone managed to find an appetite somewhere as we passed around serving plates of sliced, cold turkey and thick homemade white bread for sandwiches. I put some cranberries in mine, and was just barely able to eat it without the red juice dripping too much. Another piece of pie for all topped off the meal.

"Well, it's a long drive to Excelsior and it's already dark," said Ethel as she gathered up her girls with their dolls, as did Aunt Marion. Children were bundled into leggings, coats, hats, and mittens. The men went out to warm up the cars. Lap robes were wrapped around the girls to keep them warm on the ride home.

Good-byes were repeated all around with many compliments to all who contributed to the sumptuous Christmas dinner, especially to Mother, who obviously had prepared so ably. Aunt Susan gave me a loving hug as she left. It felt good to be enfolded in her ample arms. It was like a message that said, "You are part of us. You are family." Funny, because Aunt Susan wasn't born into this family either, but she belonged. Like me.

When everyone was gone, Mother picked up a pile of soiled linen napkins and tossed them down the clothes chute in the hallway. She returned to the kitchen and sank onto a chair near piles of clean dishes on the table. I noticed that even when Mother was tired, she was beautiful.

"I think these dishes can wait until tomorrow to be put away." Then she looked at me and said, "It's time for you to go to bed, Amy, and me too. But first, tell me, did you have a good Christmas?"

"Oh, Mother! It was the most wonderful day of my life. I didn't know Christmases could be like this. It was—" I searched for that new word I had learned at church—"it was divine!" Then, not wanting to bring the conversation to a close, I said, "Burton says trains and Tinker Toys are for boys, but that's okay, cuz I really like 'em too."

"Maybe he's just a little jealous. You didn't have very many things before, but we can make up for that now. And as for girls and trains, there was a time when men said women could never drive cars, but now many do, including me. Things change."

Dad, who had been scattering the fire in the fireplace, now chuckled as he came into the kitchen and winked at me. I had heard how Mother insisted the salesman teach her to drive when they bought the last car. He was quite reluctant and probably scared, but the sale of the car depended on his lessons.

After arranging my many toys and gifts, I selected a new favorite doll to take to bed. Mother came to tuck me in, and my first real Christmas was over.

But when the room was dark, I could not fall asleep. Underneath my happiness, some things were bothering me. How had it happened that I lived in Nesbitt luxury while my brother and orphaned friends lived with so little? Only a short time ago, I slept with Elsie and Martha, struggling for enough space in a small bed. Tonight I slept in my own bedroom, in my own big bed, holding tight to a beautiful new doll. I remembered Mary holding the baby Jesus doll at church last night. Christmas was about baby Jesus, who didn't even have a bed as nice as those in the orphanage. There were so many things I didn't understand. I began to softly hum the song we had learned for the program....

>*Be near me, Lord Jesus; I ask Thee to stay*
>*Close by me forever, and love me, I pray.*
>*Bless all the dear children in Thy tender care,*
>*And take us to heaven to live with Thee there.*

TEN

The Horses One Cold Night

I heard Dad return through the basement door and then come up the stairs into the kitchen after evening milking. I noticed he was still wearing his heavy outdoor clothes as he set the pail of warm milk in the sink. He looked concerned.

"What's the matter, John?" Mother asked.

"It's gotten pretty cold out there...awfully cold. I'm worried about the colts out in the hay field."

"What are you going to do?" Mother began straining the milk into glass jars to put into the refrigerator.

"I guess I'll walk out and take a look. Maybe bring them up to the barn."

"May I go with you?" I asked.

"Amy, it's too cold. I heard it might get down to 40 below zero tonight."

"I'll dress warm, and I won't say a word if I get cold... PLEEEZE, Dad...I can hurry and get ready."

"Well, okay." Dad nodded his approval.

I put a second sweater over the one I already wore, and pulled snowpants on top of my overalls. Mother produced a pair of Dad's big wool socks to go over my shoes before I put on my four buckle white overshoes. After buttoning up my jacket and tugging a cap down over my ears and forehead, Mother tied a scarf around my face so only my eyes could be seen.

"Ready, Dad!" My voice was a bit muffled behind the scarf.

He laughed when he saw how bundled up I was. "If the horses would wear clothes like that I'd never have to worry about them."

Since last summer I hadn't spent much time outside with Dad. I missed being at his side as he attended to farm business. For almost nine months this man had become my father, and I loved being with him.

Dad pulled the earflaps down on his cap and put on his big leather mitts with the wool liners. We went out through the basement and headed across the yard to the pasture with Jack at Dad's heels. A nearly full moon silhouetted everything black against a snowy white background. The barn and silo stood dark with white roofs; shiny icicles trimmed the edge of the eaves. With no wind, the windmill was silently still.

We were well into January, but there had been only a few inches of snow this winter, just enough to use the sleigh runners under the hayrack for bringing in hay from the field stacks. The tracks were plain to follow and made walking easy. As a farmer, used to rough paths and plowed fields, Dad always walked with a steady, easy gait.

"It's important to walk easy in such cold weather," he explained. "It can hurt your lungs if you breathe too fast, and you don't want to work up a sweat unless you want to freeze to death."

This was the first real Dad I'd ever had. He was a quiet, gentle man. We didn't usually talk a lot, but I was comfortable just being with him.

Even through the scarf, the raw air made the hairs in my nose prickle. I kept my hand in my pockets, but it might have been easier to walk with so many clothes if I would have swung my arms a bit.

"Did you ever freeze your hands or feet, Dad?"

"Yes. I did once."

"How did you do it?"

"Years ago, before cars and trucks, delivery wagons were pulled by horses. So were city street cars and carriages. I used to haul loads of hay to the horse barns in Minneapolis in an open wagon, or sleigh if we had snow."

"Could you make that trip in one day?"

"Only if I got started about 4 a.m. I'd cover myself with hay going in, but coming home was harder. It was dark by late afternoon, and the sleigh was empty. And if there was a wind, oh, my, it got bitterly cold."

"Why did you go?"

"I had to. I had to make a living. I'd ride in that sleigh until I was so cold I couldn't stand it. Then I'd jump off and run alongside until I was too tired to run anymore."

"Were the horses tired too?"

"I suppose so. But they knew there was feed and a warm barn waiting for them. They never forgot the way home."

Dad continued with his story. "One afternoon on my return, I was in such a hurry I ran too much and got too sweaty. Then, of course, when I returned to sitting in the sleigh, I really got a chill. Enough to freeze all the toes on my right foot."

"Did they hurt bad?"

"When I got home and they were thawing out, let's say it wasn't very comfortable."

The snow crunched under our boots as we walked. We heard a haunting train whistle a long way off—the sound carried clearly in the dry, cold air. A neighbor's dog howled at the moon. Good old Jack pricked up his ears, made a soft little growl, but stayed close to Dad.

We trudged across the empty oat field and I could see a haystack loom darkly on a small rise in the middle of an adjacent field.

"Remember how hot it was when we stacked that hay?" I

said.

"I certainly do. But it wasn't as bad as in the drought years."

I had heard plenty about that difficult time.

Last summer I had helped drive the horses, Jud and Dan, to mow and rake hay while Dad and Walter stacked what was already dry. Dad made the first round to open the field, then he let me cut most of the remaining field. I felt so proud holding those reins. But sometimes I thought the horses could almost do it alone because they seemed to know what they were doing more than I did. It had been incredibly hot riding 'round and 'round the field in the sun and dust, often over 100 degrees. How different from tonight.

"I don't see Prince and Lady yet," I said a bit worried.

"They must be really close to the haystack," Dad replied. Then Jack gave a little, "Yip." Sure enough, as we got nearer we could see their dark forms nearly under the hay. They had actually rubbed themselves into the side of the stack.

The horses' breath hung in clouds around their heads and the hairs around their muzzles and nostrils were covered with white frost. They looked at us as though surprised but made no effort to come to us. Dad walked over and began stroking their muzzles and patting their necks. He ran his mittened-hand along their backs and flanks. They had grown three-inch-long fur that stood out like velvet.

Dad was relieved. "Good. I think they look all right. They have plenty to eat from the haystack and snow for water. I guess we'll leave 'em here."

"Don't you think they're cold? Wouldn't they be better off in the barn with Jud and Dan?"

"No. Since they've been out all fall and winter they've grown used to the weather. See how thick and long this hair is? We keep Jud and Dan in the barn because we use them to haul the hay and straw in to the cows. They haven't grown heavy coats like this." Dad stroked the horses' muzzles again before we turned to start for home.

Prince gave a little whinny as though to say, "Good-bye," but both horses stayed under the overhang of the haystack.

"You sure like horses, don't you, Dad?"

"Well, I've worked with horses all my life. I think we understand each other."

I knew Dad preferred to handle the horses while Walter ran the tractor when there was field work to do. Dad moved at his characteristic steady pace, never making sudden movements, or hard jerking on the bits. "Gee" and "Haw" meant right and left. A light tug on the reins and a slap on the back meant "step it up."

"Yes. I like the horses. But work horses like mine are being replaced by machines, and I suppose that will be better. I've worked these same fields for about fifty years with horses. First with my father, and then for myself."

I remembered how Dad had told me that soil could get overused. "Fifty years? Gosh, I'd think the dirt would be worn out by now," I said, showing off that I had learned a lot about farming.

Dad chuckled. "Well, it doesn't wear out if it's worked right. That's why we spread the manure on it to fertilize. We try to put back as much as we take out."

"So it'll last forever?"

"It should…but I'm afraid the city will swallow it up. Oh, not in my lifetime, but maybe in yours."

I was walking behind Dad as we came back into the farm yard. It had been a pleasant outing. Dad and Jack headed into the basement, but I paused a few moments, looking up into the starry sky. Its vast beauty made me think of lines from the Christmas program,

The stars in the sky looked down where He lay . . .

and,

*I love Thee, Lord Jesus, look down from the sky,
and stay by my cradle till morning is nigh.*

I realized right then that someone must be looking after those horses out in the pasture. Of course, Dad was. But maybe Jesus was too.

Dad's head appeared from the doorway. "Amy," he called. "Thought you were right behind me. Better come in."

In the basement we took off our layers of outdoor clothes. Dad had little ice balls in his mustache. When he pulled his cap off, static electricity snapped and made his hair stand on end. He pulled a big blue handkerchief out of his pocket and blew his nose.

Mother looked down the stairwell and greeted us. "Well, look at the rosy cheeks! I can tell by your smiles everything must be all right. How about some hot chocolate to warm you up?"

As she heated the milk, old Jack was already in his favorite place licking his feet. His work and ours was done for the day.

ELEVEN

The French Sisters

I loved to watch Mother sitting at her vanity in her pink dressing gown preparing herself for the day. First, she brushed waist-length, gray hair until it was shiny and smooth. Then she began rolling it up into a neat bun held in place with hair pins. A fine hairnet completed her always tidy appearance. She told me the beautiful, silver, hand-held mirror and brush set always arranged neatly on her dresser were wedding gifts from Dad.

Just a touch of powder and rouge made her milky white skin look soft and smooth as pink rose petals. The same rouge was used to color her lips. A little spray of lilac cologne and she was ready to get dressed. *I have such a beautiful mother,* I thought as I watched.

She wore a dress with hose every day. Hanging in her closet were what she called house dresses, second-best dresses for things like shopping, and best dresses for special occasions. Always the lady, my mother wouldn't have dreamed of going out in public without gloves and a hat. But whether in a house dress or in her finest, Mother always looked like she just stepped out of a magazine.

In the corner of her bedroom was a lady's writing desk, where Mother spent a great deal of time writing each day.

There were always thank-you cards to write and longer correspondence for friends far away.

One morning while watching Mother go through her routine, I fiddled idly with things in her desk. I admired a green jade inkwell with its matching pen, and the green jade rocking horse with blotting paper on the bottom to soak up excess ink. Numerous cubby holes held stationery, envelopes, stamps, and old letters. Curiosity kept me snooping. Opening a small drawer below the cubbies I found a picture of two attractive young girls in a dainty silver frame.

"Mother, who's this?" I asked, staring at the girls dressed in white lacy dresses, satin sashes tied around their waists. Long blonde curls fell below their shoulders.

Mother looked a little surprised. "Oh! Well. They are two French sisters."

"Why do you have their picture?" I inquired.

After a pause Mother replied, "Well, when we were first investigating the possibility of...adopting a child, the adoption agency asked if we would be interested in these two girls in France. Then one of them became ill, so they were unable to come to the United States. So you see, it worked out for the best because we got you!" But something in her voice sounded strange.

Mother tried to hide embarrassment, but I saw her face was a bit flushed as she left the room and headed toward the kitchen.

"Oh." My heart sank. I was not their first choice. *I was not their first choice!*

The French sisters look so feminine, I thought. *Like real ladies.* I shoved the picture back in the drawer and tried to act normal, but I felt like I'd been punched in the stomach. It took all the control I could muster to hold back tears. Passing by the dresser mirror, I caught a sight of myself in overalls—not at all like the dainty, lacy French sisters. *They'd probably never spend time out with the cows and chickens*, I thought. *The French sisters are dainty and beautiful like Mother. Dad says I'm going to be a large woman.*

"I'm going outside," I mumbled to Mother as I passed through the kitchen.

Dad had hung a swing for me in a big, old oak tree in back of the house. It was a good place to think.

The weather was warming up. Spring was in the air. I slowly kicked my feet, making the swing glide gently back and forth.

The French sisters are prettier than me, and I bet they are smarter, too. Why am I always second best?

Now the tears slid down my cheeks. *Why did Mother keep their picture? Wasn't I good enough?*

Of course I was very grateful that they had adopted me. But it hurt to know there had been someone else Mother and Dad prepared their hearts for, and probably still had a place there for...not one girl, but two! I had so many questions I wanted to ask them, but then they would think I was ungrateful and didn't want to be their little girl.

A crushing loneliness came over me. If I wasn't really wanted here, maybe it would be better to be back at the orphanage where there were lots of girls to play with and I'd get to see Harold.

I spent all morning outside on the swing imagining the French sisters expertly playing the baby grand piano in the living room for Mother and Dad. In January, my parents had enthusiastically placed me in piano lessons. Within a few weeks it became obvious I had absolutely no aptitude for the piano. In fact, I hated it. My piano teacher expected me to remember what various notes were from one week to the next, and count time too! How do people count and play at the same time? I tried to keep my frustration from showing too much, but unsuccessfully. Surely, the French sisters are talented pianists.

"Time to come in for lunch," Mother called.

Once at the table, head forward, I played with my food, pushing it around on the plate with my fork. I couldn't look up at Mother.

"What's the matter, Amy?" asked Dad.

"I'm not hungry."

"Are you sick?"

"She's okay, John," answered Mother. "Sometimes girls don't feel like eating. I'm sure she'll be hungry by suppertime. Right, Amy?"

"Uh-huh. May I please be excused?"

"Yes, dear."

I went to my bedroom, picked up my baby doll, and headed outside again. Even a doll was someone to hug and talk to, even if she didn't have any answers. Swinging back and forth in the fresh air with her under one arm cleared my thinking some.

Flowerbeds around the house showed spring's progress. Mother was teaching me the names of flowers as each one appeared. Crocuses had been first, probably glad to be above ground after a long cold winter. Next to come were yellow daffodils. And now the lilacs bushes gently shook their deliciously fragrant purple blooms in the gentle breeze. If I looked over my shoulder, I could see apple trees that resembled big, pink powder puffs.

Mother spends a lot of time making this a beautiful yard, I thought.

"Amy," Mother called, "will you please come in? I can use your help."

I took my time getting off the swing and dragged my feet as I walked to the house. After putting my baby doll back in the bedroom, I went into the kitchen, where Mother seemed to be assembling various kitchen utensils.

"How would you like to help me make some oatmeal-raisin

cookies?" she asked.

"I don't know how," I murmured. *Don't know if I want to either. Those French girls are probably good cooks too.*

"Wash your hands, and I'll tell you what ingredients we need."

At the sink, I stalled as long as I could, playing with the soap bubbles. Finally, I wiped my hands and waited for instructions.

"Measuring spoons are by the bowl. We need 1 teaspoon of salt…1/2 teaspoon baking soda…1 teaspoon cinnamon…" Mother continued dictating the things we needed as I measured them into a large bowl. Mixing the firm dough made my arms ache, so Mother took a turn now and then. We dropped spoonfuls of dough onto cookie sheets in neat rows, all the same distance apart

When the first batch was baked and cooled, Mother poured me a glass of cold milk to accompany a couple big, fat, warm cookies.

"Yum. They're so good."

"I'm glad you like them. Oatmeal-raisin has always been a favorite of mine too. We could do a lot of baking together, Amy, if you'd like. Would you like to learn how to bake bread?"

"Well, I guess so. I love your bread."

"Let's wrap a few cookies in some waxed paper. You can take a snack out to Dad and Walter. I just saw them walking toward the machine shed."

"Okay."

Walking to the shed, I realized I would never have the courage to bring up the subject of the French sisters to my Mother. Nor would Mother ever bring up the topic, either.

Twelve

Horse Play

"How many times have you been told to close the barn door, Amy?" Dad's gray eyes looked as stormy as the weather. It had been raining for a few days and that meant the men couldn't work in the fields. The hay was nearly ready to be cut. There was always plenty to do on rainy days, though. A fence to mend or buildings to fix, but too many rainy days made everyone a little edgy.

Dad seldom scolded me, but when he did, I felt crushed. My mouth gaped open for a moment. My mind was like a tornado. I couldn't think of what to say.

"The horses got in the barn and ate too much grain," he continued. "I'm afraid they may be sick."

"But Dad, I didn't leave the door open. I haven't even been to the barn this morning. I've been in my room making doll clothes."

"Well, someone did, and Walter says it wasn't him." Dad sat down for dinner. He spoke more gently now. "You know we must be careful to close that door because horses will overeat on oats—just like kids with candy."

"I promise I didn't do it." Anger was rising inside me for being accused of doing something I didn't do. Suddenly I didn't have much of an appetite.

Dad wasn't finished. "Horses get colic. Maybe you don't know that horses can't vomit, so they can't get rid of too much food. If they show signs of discomfort, we'll have to give them some colic remedy…may even need to walk them for a long time to work it off."

A small bin was kept near the horse stalls with a few days' supply of oats. When the horses were working hard they were given about a quart of oats morning and evening, along with all the hay they wanted. When they weren't working they were turned out to pasture, where they grazed on grass.

After dinner I went to my room to continue making doll clothes and also think things over. It hurt that Dad thought I had been irresponsible. I loved him so much and tried to do things as well as I could to please him. Now he doubted my honesty.

The next morning Dad announced that, fortunately, the horses didn't get colic. He must have found them in the barn before they had eaten too much. But I was convinced he still thought I was the one who had been careless with the door.

The rain continued the next day.

Later in the week Mother got a phone call from Alice Johnson, who lived about a mile away.

"Ida, there's a team of bay horses in our yard, and I think

they're yours."

"Oh, my stars! I wonder how they got out? Thanks, Alice, John will come and get them right away."

"That's okay," Alice replied. "It happens to everyone with horses once in a while. No harm done."

Mother hung up the phone and turned to me. "Amy, go tell Dad the horses are at Johnsons'. The fence must be down somewhere. There are so many cars on the road nowadays, a loose horse might run out and cause an accident. I guess when horses don't have work to do, they feel kind of frisky."

I found Dad and Walter repairing machinery in the barn, since it was too wet to work in the field. When I told Dad about the phone call, he was pretty upset.

"I know they didn't break the fence, and I can see the big gate from here. Was the little gate by our house closed when you came over?"

"Yes, Dad, and the spring keeps it shut."

"I don't understand it," he said. "Well, go down to the barn and get a lead rope. We'll drive over and bring them back."

It was our team in the Johnsons' yard, all right. Dad chatted with Alice for a moment, thanking her for the call. "I'm sorry, Alice. I haven't figured out how they got out."

"That's okay," she replied. "But if they'd trampled my flowerbeds they'd have been in *real* trouble."

With a lead rope on Dan, Jud followed with no trouble. Dad drove slowly, and I held the rope out the window. The horses seemed to have had their little fun so were willing to go home.

"We can't let this happen again," Dad warned.

Somehow I still felt like he thought it was my fault.

The French sisters wouldn't be out in the barn, so they wouldn't get blamed for leaving gates open, I couldn't help but think. *They looked too prissy to be in overalls and rubber boots.*

A few days later, Uncle Knute called, seeking Dad's opinion on various farm matters. Always liking an opportunity to entertain, Mother invited Knute and his family for dinner. I was glad to hear that Cousin Burton would be coming. I decided to confide in him. Burton seemed to be a reasonable person, and being two years older, he tended to have a different perspective on things.

When they arrived, the men settled right into conversation in the living room, and Mother and Aunt Annie put the finishing touches on dinner. I saw my chance.

"Burton, let's go outside until dinner is ready," I said.

As we wandered around the yard, I told Burton about the horse escapades.

"Last week, Dad thought I left the barn door open. But that morning I had been doing things in my room and I hadn't even been in the barn. I feel so bad he doesn't believe me."

"Maybe he just didn't know who else to blame, and he was pretty worried about the horses. Don't you worry about it," said Burton in his level-headed way.

I took a deep breath and brought up what I was most worried about. "Burton, do you think Mother and Dad are unhappy with me…and will send me back to the orphanage?"

He stopped and stared at me. "NO! They adopted you. They are your parents for life."

"Do you really think so?"

"I'm positive."

Burton made me feel a lot better. It sure was good to talk about things with him.

"Amy! Burton! It's time to come in for dinner," Mother called.

As usual, we sat in the dining room with our company. And, as usual, Mother had made a wonderful meal. Carrots and potatoes surrounded the tender pot roast. Of course, everyone raved about her apple pie with its flaky crust.

As I lay in bed that night, I tried to sort out my recent feelings: *Life here has its challenges…but it's much better than when I was a very little girl, sometimes wondering if there would be food at all. It's nice to have my own room…and relatives who live nearby. I guess Mom and Dad have done pretty much everything to make me feel like I belong.*

When the rain finally stopped, the men and the horses returned to work in the fields every day. In the welcome summer sunshine, you could almost see the corn grow.

Sundays were always days of rest. Dad fed and milked the cows but didn't do other work. After morning chores, Walter also had the day off. The horses were turned out on Saturday evening to graze. Sometimes they'd roll on the ground or kick up their heels for a good run around the pasture.

"If I hadn't seen 'em with my own eyes, I never would've believed it," I heard Dad say as I entered the kitchen for breakfast on Sunday.

"Amy, what do you think I saw?" asked Dad.

"I dunno." I shrugged.

"Just as I came around the corner of the barn, I saw the two horses at the door." He chuckled. "Dan was working on the wooden latch with his teeth, so I stood still and watched. Dan got the latch unfastened and pulled the door open and was about to go in when I whistled. Both horses turned their heads, lifted their tails, and scampered off like a couple of naughty boys caught at their trick."

"Really, Dad? That's amazing." This was welcome news.

Dad sat down to his bacon, eggs, and fried potatoes. "I already fixed the barn door so they won't be able to do that again."

"Do you suppose they found their own way to get out of the pasture, too?" Mother wondered as she poured steaming coffee into Dad's cup.

He added a spoonful of sugar to his coffee and stirred thoughtfully. "I don't see how. I've never found a gate open, and if the fence was down that day, the cows would've gotten out, too."

One evening, a few days later, this second puzzle was also solved. Again, the culprit was Dan. Dad and I were sitting on the porch after dinner enjoying the cool breeze after a hot day. We noticed that Dan and Jud were ambling around on the other side of the fence near the small gate. Even though this gate had a strong spring to keep it shut, we saw Dan pull the gate open with his chin. It snapped shut several times, but finally he succeeded in holding it open long enough for Jud to walk through. After several more tries, Dan managed to hold the gate open enough to get his own shoulder into the opening and then slip his whole body through. The gate slammed shut behind him.

I could hardly believe what we had just seen. When Dad gave a whistle, Dan and Jud kicked up their heels as if to say, "Catch us if you can."

They trotted along the fence, but by running as fast as I could, I managed to head them off while Dad unfastened the spring and left the gate open. The horses turned back and went into the pasture without causing any more trouble.

Panting, I returned to Dad. "Those dumb horses," I gasped.

"Not so dumb," Dad said. "Pretty clever, actually. But we can't let them get away with this. I need to devise something to make the gate more secure."

Dad attached to the gate a leather strap with a harness buckle on the end to fasten into the wire fence. It was a little inconvenient to always buckle and unbuckle the gate, but it was better than chasing horses.

Of course, the best part was that Dad now believed I had not been irresponsible, and I had told him the truth.

Thirteen

Vacation Bible School

My memorable third-grade year, which had brought so many changes into my life, slid into another summer, and then, too quickly, another school year.

By now, I had become fairly accustomed to life as a Nesbitt. On the last day of fourth grade, the weather was already warm, which meant it was strawberry season. Mother and I again picked the wonderful red fruit from the raised beds in the corner of the yard. There was nothing better to eat in the whole world than Mother's shortcake, piled high with sliced strawberries and topped with freshly whipped cream. I had just polished off a good helping of this dessert and continued to sit contentedly at the table as I anticipated another summer of freedom on the farm.

Suddenly, Mother interrupted my thoughts. "The church is offering Vacation Bible School this summer. I think it would be a good idea for you to go."

I sensed a door closing on my plans. "Bible School? How long does it last?" I asked skeptically.

"It's four hours each morning…it's just two weeks. You'll sing songs, do crafts, and learn Bible verses."

"Awww. Do I have to go? I was looking forward to helping Dad around the farm."

"You'll have all afternoon to help. I'm sure there'll be other children you know from school. I'd really like you to go. I think you'll enjoy it."

I sensed the decision had been made and my objections would get me nowhere. "Well, okay," I said with little enthusiasm.

During one of her visits last winter, Aunt Susan had brought me a big, red book of Bible stories written for children. I valued the book a lot, particularly because it was a gift from Aunt Susan, from whom I felt genuine love. She never failed to enfold me in a huge hug whenever she arrived...and then another one when she left. I had been intrigued by the book's pictures accompanying each story, and had spent several winter evenings scrutinizing the pictures and sometimes reading the stories, as my reading skills had improved quite a bit during fourth grade. Sometimes Mother or Dad would read me a story. Those were special times between us. With this Bible knowledge, I wondered why I needed to have any more.

Later, when I learned Mrs. Swenson would be my VBS teacher, I felt a little better about going. I had come to know Agnes Swenson quite well. Not only had she been my Sunday school teacher during the past year, but I also associated her with good memories of the Christmas program she had directed my first Christmas here. In Sunday school, Mrs. Swenson had encouraged friendly competition to help us memorize the Ten Commandments and the books of the Bible. Each week I proudly showed my parents the lengthening line of stars charting my progress.

Mostly, Mrs. Swenson and I had become friends at the general store she and her husband owned. The store was about a quarter of a mile from our farm. I often went there with Mother or Dad to pick up various small items between our regular but longer trips to Hall's Mercantile in town, where we bought larger quantities from their greater variety.

I always enjoyed visiting with Mrs. Swenson. Dad, her husband, Tom, and other men discussed crops, weather, and how the Great Depression was affecting Minnesota farms and businesses. One day when we arrived at the store business was slow, as it often was, and Mrs. Swenson was sitting in a rocking chair knitting a sweater. When I admired it, she asked if I was interested in learning how to knit, and said she would be happy to teach me. We set a time to begin, and soon I was practicing basic stitches on a long, blue neck scarf.

The Swensons were about the same age as my parents, and had two grown children who lived in the East. Mrs. Swenson looked younger and more up-to-date than Mother, probably because she wore her light brown curls in a modern bob. The spicy aroma of the store seemed to linger on her as we sat side by side. It reminded me of gingerbread.

VBS, as we called it, began the following Monday. My class was made up of twelve fourth, fifth, and sixth graders. Mother was right; there were several boys and girls I knew from school in my class. Betsy Nelson, who was in my grade, motioned me to sit next to her. From that day on, Betsy and I became good friends.

After we were all seated and she had greeted us, Mrs. Swenson announced that the theme for VBS that summer was "Abba Father." That sounded strange to me. Was it even English? She had printed a Bible verse in tall letters on a large piece of white paper and hung it at the front of the classroom. It said *Romans 8:15.*

"Please sit down, class. My name is Mrs. Swenson. I'm so glad to have you here. We're going to memorize Romans 8:15

during Vacation Bible School and learn what it means. Let's read the sign in unison," she said.

We all read, "For ye have not received the spirit of bondage again to fear; but ye have received the Spirit of adoption, whereby we cry, Abba, Father."

"Isn't that a wonderful verse?" she said.

Mrs. Swenson gave us each a piece of paper with the Bible verse so we could work on memorizing it at home.

As I copied, I tried to understand the words, without much success. I was surprised to learn the Bible had something to say about adoption. Why did God want people to be adopted? After all, most people already had parents. My adoption had been a good thing, but, to be really honest way down deep, I'd rather have been born into a family that loved me and wanted to keep me from the start. It had been no fun being an orphan. And then becoming part of a new family had called for many adjustments, both emotional and physical. Did the verse mean that other people should want to be adopted, too? *And what does "Abba" mean?* I wondered.

With our writing completed Mrs. Swenson asked, "If you were going to draw a picture of 'Abba Father,' what would you draw?"

I was baffled. All I could think of was my own dad. I imagined trying to draw him with his mustache and wearing overalls.

"Betsy," our teacher said, "what would you draw?"

"Well, I guess I'd draw Him in a beautiful white robe, and a crown on His head, and with light all around."

I wondered what in the world she'd draw her dad like that for. Mrs. Swenson was asking other children the same question.

"Why would you draw your dad like that? Wearing a robe and all?" I whispered to Betsy.

"Not my dad! Abba Father is God!" she replied.

"Oh!"

Mrs. Swenson was speaking to everyone again. She told us that in Hebrew, *Abba* meant "Daddy," or "Papa."

"Think of a little child running to his father, calling him 'Daddy,'" Mrs. Swenson continued. "The name helps us know that God is tender and loving toward his children."

When it was time to draw, Mrs. Swenson distributed crayons and paper. The assignment asked us to draw Abba Father. At least I knew what God looked like. His name helps us to know that He is tender and loving to his children.

That had cleared up one part of the verse, but not all. I doodled with a figure like Betsy had described. Soon it was time to put the crayons away. I wasn't ready to move on. Things seemed to be moving too quickly. I had a lot of questions. Finally, I folded my paper in half twice and didn't turn it in when they were collected.

Mrs Swenson moved over to the piano and told us to open our songbooks to page 58. As she played, we sang all four verses of "He Leadeth Me." The chorus after each verse was,

He leadeth me, He leadeth me,
By His own hand He leadeth me:
His faithful foll'wer I would be,
For by His hand He leadeth me.

We went outside for cookies and lemonade and a short recess. Betsy and I took our snack and memory verse papers across the church yard and sat under a shade tree. As we munched sugar cookies, we began reciting the verse to each other.

Suddenly, two boys from the class walked over and hovered above us.

"Amy Nesbitt," Donald, the biggest one, sneered. "Whata you care about memorizing a Bible verse about adoption? The rest of us kids have lived here all our lives. You show up and get adopted to the Nesbitts."

"Yeah," chimed in Buddy, his sidekick with dirty overalls. "Now you live in the big, fancy house on the hill, while we still live down in the river bottoms. You must really think you're somethin', huh? You have it pretty good."

Shocked at this unexpected verbal attack, I started to cry.

"Aw, look at the crybaby," teased Donald.

"Don't listen to them," said Betsy, taking my hand. "Come on. Recess is almost over; let's go back inside." I wiped my tears as we quickly walked across the grass to the church. The boys didn't follow. When we were on the front steps, Betsy stopped and turned to me. "They're just jealous, you know. Wanna know a secret?"

I sniffled and nodded.

"I'm adopted too," she whispered. "But my parents got me when I was just a little baby, so most people don't know."

"Really?" I was pleased to have something so important in common with my friend.

"Donald and Buddy are just bullies; don't listen to them," she consoled me.

Entering the classroom, I saw Mrs. Swenson arranging some pictures. I went over to her and spoke in a soft voice. "Mrs. Swenson, I don't understand the memory verse about adoption and Abba Father. It's really confusing to me."

She looked at me with kind interest. "I think you'll understand more as the week goes by. But I'd be happy to talk to you about it sooner. Would you like to walk over to the store this afternoon? We can have some lemonade and a little chat."

While we were outside, Mrs. Swenson had arranged our chairs in a semicircle. During the rest of the morning, she presented the first part of the story of Joseph from the Bible using a flannel-covered board. Betsy sat next to me and we held hands. I had read this story at home in my book from Aunt Susan, but seeing all the characters appear and disappear on the board gave me a much better understanding of what it was about. The first picture was Joseph wearing his coat of many colors. Mrs. Swenson asked us if our mothers ever made a shirt or dress for us. I thought about several dresses Mother had sewn for me in the past two years.

Joseph's home life was not good because his brothers hated him. When Joseph shared his dreams that one day his family would bow down to him, they were furious. Mrs. Swenson put up pictures of the brothers tending sheep, and alongside was a pit. She told us how the brothers plotted to kill Joseph. "But God had other plans," she said. "He provided a caravan of traders who took Joseph off to Egypt."

As I watched her put up the traders with their camels, I couldn't help but feel compassion for Joseph, who had received such unkind treatment.

"Joseph was separated from his father, who loved him dearly. But Joseph had another Father. His heavenly Abba Father, who loved him perfectly, protected him, and blessed him in Egypt beyond what he could have imagined."

I was eager to see the pictures of Joseph in Egypt, but Mrs. Swenson said this was where she would end for today. Tomorrow and all through the week, she would continue the story.

After singing, "God Will Take Care of You," we were dismissed.

"I'll sit by you tomorrow," Betsy whispered.

"Okay, thanks Betsy. See you."

Mrs. Swenson continued playing the piano and the first morning was over.

Fourteen

The Adoption Club

After lunch, with Mother's permission, I walked down the dirt road to Swenson's General Store. The familiar little bell above the door rang as I entered this friendly atmosphere that smelled of cinnamon, cloves, and allspice. Walking toward the back the smell was of grain specially mixed with molasses for horses. On the sides, shelves were stacked from floor to ceiling with all manner of goods and staples. That's where I saw Mr. Swenson, arranging bags of flour. There wasn't anyone else in the store.

"Good afternoon, Amy," he greeted. "Agnes is expecting you. She's upstairs finishing up the lunch dishes."

"Hello, Mr. Swenson. Mother gave me a short list of things to pick up for her when I head home." I handed him the list. "Is it okay if I go up now?"

"Sure. I'll have these things ready for you when you come down. In fact, I'll collect them right away."

I climbed the steps to the small quarters where the couple lived. Mrs. Swenson was wiping wet hands on her apron. She greeted me with a big smile, poured a glass of lemonade for each of us, and we sat down together at her kitchen table.

On the table were neat stacks of figures I recognized as the cutouts for the flannelboard story of Joseph. They gave me a place to start the conversation. One thing I liked about Mrs. Swenson was that she let me talk a lot, and she always seemed to be listening.

"I loved hearing you tell the story of Joseph with the flannelboard," I said. "I've read the story in a book at home. His coat of many colors made me think of the nice clothes Mother's made for me. The way his brothers treated him...that was cruel. He sure didn't have a good family life, and then he was separated from his family for a long, long time." With this last sentence, a thought of my own brother flashed into my mind.

"Yes, he was. I'm glad you know the story. Joseph is a fine example of how much God loves us and how He takes care of us through good times and bad. As you know, the story gets even better when we learn that, not only did God protect Joseph, but preserved the entire Hebrew people through him."

"That's because He's Abba Father," I said, recalling the memory verse. "But what about the word *adoption* in today's verse? That's what I don't understand. I already was adopted. I've been getting used to having new parents for two years...and now there's more family business to take care of?"

Mrs. Swenson smiled, as if to speak, but I continued. "I want to tell you something...privately." I hesitated, then went on. "You know I love and appreciate my dad and my mother. But I think one father is about all I can handle right now, because...well, they're awfully hard to please sometimes. And... also, Dad doesn't always believe me, even when I tell the truth." My chin quivered and my voice got shaky.

"What do you mean, Amy?"

My words tumbled forth. "Well, my grades in school aren't particularly good sometimes. They want me to get good grades all the time. And Mother tells me to 'act more like a lady.' She always reminds me to 'sit like a lady,' and 'stand like a lady,' and 'walk like a lady.' And then, about not believing me, the horses got into the barn a few weeks ago and Dad blamed me for

85

leaving the barn door open. Then, another day, the horses got out of the pasture and went all the way over to the Johnsons' a mile away. Dad thought I left the gate open, but I didn't. He found out later that one of the horses learned how to open the latch and I didn't do it after all. But I hate being blamed for things I didn't do."

Mrs. Swenson gave my hand a pat. "That reminds me about tomorrow's part of Joseph's story. Have you read how Joseph was falsely accused and even put in prison for years over something he didn't do? Amy, your dad, as a farmer, was logically trying to figure out how the horses could open a barn door or a gate. Again, Abba Father knows your heart and applauds your sincere efforts. But the good news is, Abba Father knew the truth all along."

"Abba Father believed me?"

"Of course," said Mrs. Swenson. "And when you feel your parents aren't pleased with you, just remember they are only trying to encourage you to do the best you can."

These were comforting thoughts needing more consideration. But I rushed on. "There's something else about being part of my family that bothers me." Now tears began to form in my eyes and threatened to spill down my cheeks. "Before the Nesbitts adopted me, they were going to adopt some French girls, two sisters. One got sick, so they couldn't come to this country. That means I...wasn't their first choice."

Mrs. Swenson was consoling. "It must have hurt when you learned about them. But, Amy, I'm positive the Nesbitts are glad it worked out the way it did. Surely they're happy you're their daughter. And think about this: you are always Abba Father's first choice. In the Bible, Jesus, God's Son, says, '*Let the little children come to Me, and do not forbid them; for of such is the kingdom of heaven.*' Jesus loved little children, and still does. I can imagine children sitting on his lap."

Now tears did run down my cheeks. "He must be very

kind, and you are too, Mrs. Swenson. I really appreciate your words...only there's still one more thing that really upsets me. Something I think about almost every day...." I felt like I needed more air and began taking big gulps.

"Amy, my dear," Mrs. Swenson put her arms around me. "I'm sorry you're troubled. Here, try taking a drink of lemonade. Now, how about some deep, slow breaths. There now, tell me what else is bothering you."

"I...have...a...brother named...Harold." After a few more breaths I was able to continue. "He'll be old enough soon to leave the orphanage and get a job...or maybe he already has. I guess because he was that old, the state said it was best for Harold to stay there, so he probably never was adopted."

"You've never heard from your brother since you left the orphanage?"

"No. And I...don't...know where to write...or anything." I started to cry again.

"Have you talked to your mother about this?"

"Only once. Mother said the state felt a clean break between us was best, but maybe I could get some information sometime...maybe when I'm older. Mother asked me not to talk about it anymore. She said she and Dad would try to be the best family to me that they could."

"I'm sure the Nesbitts are indeed the best parents they know how to be. I think they would do anything for you. Amy, I don't want to give you false hope, because you may or may not see your brother again, but I do know one thing for a fact, Jesus wants to be your brother, too."

"My brother? How?" I asked, still sniffling.

"Look here in my Bible at Mark 3:35." She quickly turned pages. "Jesus says, *'For whosoever shall do the will of God, the same is my brother, and my sister, and mother.'*" If we do the will of God, our adopted brother, Jesus, is with us all the time.'"

"What do you mean, 'adopted brother'?"

"To explain, I'll let you in on tomorrow's memory verse for VBS." Mrs. Swenson again opened her black Bible, this time to one of several places marked with bookmarks. She read, *"'I will be a Father to you and ye shall be my sons and daughters,' saith the Lord Almighty in Second Corinthians 6:18."*

"Oh! If we are sons and daughters of God, then Jesus is our brother!"

"You're absolutely right. Let's go back to the verse in Mark. Notice that it says, '...*whosoever shall do the will of God, the same is my brother.*' That brings me to—" Mrs. Swenson's eyes twinkled—"telling you that *I* am adopted! Well, not exactly the same way you are. I was raised by my birth parents, but I have been adopted into the family of God. In fact, everyone who believes Jesus is God's Son, sent to earth to save us from our sins, can be adopted into God's family. That's God's will for us. I like to call it joining the club—The Adoption Club! Those who join all become adopted children of Abba Father. And as His children, we are His heirs. That means we receive His blessings on this earth, and also have the promise of eternal life with Him in Heaven. Doesn't that sound like a good life?"

Suddenly, I felt like the whole world around me was much more clear. I had known about and felt God's love before, but never like this. Then a thought worried me. "Mrs. Swenson, am I in The Adoption Club? Is Abba Father my Father? Am I in His family?"

"There's only one way to be sure about that," she said. "I think you've heard the verse, '*I am the way, the truth, and the life; no man cometh unto the Father, but by me.*' That's *John 14:6*. Another verse says that Jesus stands at the door of our hearts, knocking, patiently waiting to be invited inside. Believing in Jesus and asking Him to be in our heart is the only way to know Abba Father. Jesus washes us clean from our sin by forgiving us. He's always with us to show us the way to live as part of Abba Father's family. Would you like to join right now? Would you like to ask Jesus to come into your heart?"

Mrs. Swenson took my hands in hers. "I will pray, and you can agree. Then it will be your prayer too."

"All right." I had never prayed much other than at meals and before I went to bed. Mrs. Swenson closed her eyes and began speaking to God. Her voice was the same as when she was speaking to me. "Gracious Heavenly Father, Amy comes to You today, asking to be Your child. By the blood of Your Son, Jesus, wash her sins away, and may Your Spirit dwell within her. Be her comfort, Father, especially as she grieves the loss of her brother. Be her constant companion. Teach her to love You more day by day, and to love those around her. Bless her forevermore, Father, with Your goodness. In the name of our Lord Jesus Christ, Amen."

I knew that this had been an afternoon like none other in my life. Things around me had not changed, but *I* felt different. A part of me I hadn't known existed felt alive and joyful. How could I be this peaceful after all those tears? Mrs. Swenson and I exchanged hugs, and I sincerely thanked her for her kindness. I walked home, carrying a bag with the things Mother had ordered. My status as an adopted child had been radically changed. I was a member of The Adoption Club!

I looked up. The sky had never been so blue.

Fifteen

Friendship

Mother was preparing supper when I burst into the kitchen.

"Can I invite Betsy Nelson to sleep overnight on Friday?" I asked as I put the bag from Swenson's store on the counter.

"Why, yes. That's a good idea. Betsy seems like a very nice girl." She eyed me closely. "You certainly seem excited about something."

"I am. Mrs. Swenson told me about The Adoption Club, and I want to tell Betsy about it 'cuz she's adopted too."

"The Adoption Club?"

"Yes. It's really special. It means that you're part of God's family, and Jesus is your brother. I don't understand everything about it yet, but I do know that everyone is welcome to join. Maybe people that are adopted, like me, are particularly interested in it."

"Oh," said Mother with a smile. "I'll talk to Betsy's mother tomorrow when I pick you up from Bible School, and we'll make arrangements. Would you like Betsy to stay and play on Saturday if she'd like?"

"Oh, good," I said happily as I unloaded the bag from Swenson's. "By the way, VBS is turning out to be much better than I expected...except for Donald and Buddy. They are bullies."

"What did they do?"

"Well, our Bible verse is something like, *'By the spirit of adoption we are able to call God Abba Father.'* During recess, Donald and Buddy teased me about being adopted. Betsy told me they're jealous because our house is nicer than theirs, and that they live in the river bottoms. It hurt my feelings, though, 'cuz I've been trying to fit in with the kids at school ever since I moved here."

"I'm so sorry. You were pretty quiet in the car when I drove you home this noon; now I know why. I'm glad Mrs. Swenson is your teacher and Betsy's a friend."

"Me, too! And I liked the flannelboard Bible story about Joseph, and the singing too. And now that I know Jesus is my brother and he's always with me, I feel differently about Donald and Buddy. It's like everything's changed, and I'm not afraid anymore of what they might say to me."

"Well, my stars, Amy! You're absolutely bubbling. It sounds like you learned a lot today."

"I can't wait to tell Betsy about the Adoption Club."

But on the second day of Vacation Bible School, I didn't get a chance to tell Betsy anything before Mrs. Swenson told the whole class some of the same things she had told me. After we recited yesterday's memory verse, she had us read and copy a new one:

> *"I will be a Father unto you, and ye shall be my sons and daughters,"* saith the Lord Almighty.
> —2 Corinthians 6:18

Mrs. Swenson explained, "God, our Abba Father, loves us so much that He wants everyone to have an opportunity to be adopted into His family."

I sat there smiling, already knowing about the Spirit of adoption.

"Because all people have sinned," Mrs. Swenson explained, "there's a separation between us and God, who is perfect."

"Long ago, God made a plan to fix this separation," she said as she turned to place a picture of Jesus on a cross on the flannelboard. "Instead of punishing us for our sins, God sent His perfect Son, Jesus, to pay our price with His own life. His death on the cross was the most wonderful miracle in the world because it washed away our sins. It is a gift we don't deserve."

This explanation helped me better understand what she had told me the day before.

"But," Mrs. Swenson went on, "each person needs to accept this gift individually. If it isn't accepted, if Jesus isn't believed, we miss out."

She removed the picture of the cross and replaced it with one of Jesus knocking on a door. "Jesus knocks at the door of each person's heart. By that I mean He wants to be part of our whole life. If we ask Jesus into our lives, by faith He cleanses us from sin. Then we are clean enough to become part of God's family. This is the 'Spirit of adoption' from our Bible verse," she said. "It's like joining a wonderful club forever and ever—The Adoption Club!"

The classroom was quiet. Everyone seemed to be thinking about what we had heard. Then, Mrs. Swenson sang a song.

> *"Into my heart; into my heart;*
> *come into my heart, Lord Jesus.*
> *Come in today. Come in to stay.*
> *Come into my heart, Lord Jesus."*

The room was still very quiet. Then Mrs. Swenson said, "Many years ago, I sang this song, asking Jesus to come into my life. And He did! If you want Jesus to wash your sins away so you too can be part of God's family, you can sing these same words with me. Remember, you are not singing for me. This singing is a very important prayer to Jesus." She went on to say that maybe some of us had already asked Jesus into our hearts. I knew she was thinking of me. "We only need to ask once, but it's okay to sing along if you want."

I shut my eyes and quietly sang with Mrs. Swenson. I heard other voices sing too. Best of all, I heard Betsy's voice beside me. Now Jesus was her brother too. And I was her sister. We were both in Abba Father's Adoption Club.

At recess, I ignored Donald and Buddy. They didn't pay attention to me, either.

Friday night's sleepover was the first of many fun times with Betsy that summer. I had not shared a bed since my two years with Elsie and Martha. This, of course, was much different. First of all, my Nesbitt bed was a lot bigger, and second, we two girls whispered and giggled until all hours...well, until Mother tapped on the door and insisted we get some sleep.

Several times Betsy invited me to her house, too. She lived much closer to town, not on a farm, but a neighborhood with houses nearby. Our parents knew each other from church and seemed pleased to become better acquainted. Mr. Nelson was a banker; he and Dad often talked about the economy.

When Betsy came over, we loved to pick bunches of wildflowers that grew all along the path the cows walked. When we explored in the woods, we would make up spooky stories and I would remember again how afraid I had been there once. Sometimes we helped Mother pull weeds in her flower garden that grew all around the house. It wasn't like work at all when Betsy was with me. How good it was to have a friend.

In the evenings, sometimes we read from my Bible Story book. After we read several stories, suddenly Betsy noticed how many Bible characters were not raised by their birth parents. There was Esther, an orphan who lived with her cousin Mordecai and became an important queen. We enjoyed reading the story of Moses, hidden in a basket on a river. He was found by the daughter of Pharaoh, who took him to the palace as her son. Then we read about a boy named Samuel, whose mother promised God that if she had a son, he would be given to serve Eli, the high priest.

"We know someone else who left his father," observed Betsy. "Jesus. He left His home in heaven to be a man on earth."

"And he did it for us," I said. "So we could be sisters in The Adoption Club."

Fall came quickly. I didn't mind the prospect of fifth grade too much because I still could see Betsy every day. In fact, she sat right behind me in school. In front of me was Donald Olson, of VBS.

In early August, Mother had noted I was growing like a weed, outgrowing my clothes. She made me a pretty new calico dress for the first day of school. It had little blue flowers with tiny green leaves on a tan background. As usual, she put in a deep hem so it could be lengthened as I grew. Mother was teaching me to sew; she had me put in the buttons down the back.

On the first day, Betsy and I admired both of our new dresses. I thought she looked beautiful in her new red gingham that complimented her long black wavy hair. It was tied back with a red ribbon and drawn up near the top of her head, making her big brown eyes look even bigger.

About midmorning, Miss Peterson, our teacher, told us to take out paper, pen, and ink for our penmanship lesson. We all groaned. Penmanship had never been anyone's favorite.

Our desks were bolted to the floor in straight rows. The seat of one desk was fastened to the desk of the one behind it. A space under the desktop held books, paper, pencils, crayons, and ink bottles. Everything would fit, if it were arranged carefully. Every year, as often as once a day, a desk would empty its contents onto the floor as a student tried to find an article that had slipped to the back of the space.

"As you already know, the Palmer Method has been developed so we can write beautifully and legibly," Miss Peterson said.

With a rustling of paper and uncorking of ink bottles, we prepared to practice "push-pulls" and "circles." The ink pens were difficult to handle. The metal nibs had a tendency to scratch and catch the lined paper, splattering ink. I immediately dipped my pen too deeply into the inkwell, getting ink on my fingers.

"Remember to slant your paper so that the upper left corner and the lower right corner are in a straight line with your chest," Miss Peterson instructed. "Hold your pen so that three fingers slide smoothly on the paper."

The class settled into the task of making rows of circles to perfectly fill two lines on the paper. Donald, in front of me, must have been having difficulty with his circles. He squirmed constantly, jiggling my desk. My own circles suffered from the vibration. I whispered, "Donald, sit still!"

At the sound of my voice, Donald turned around, elbow

first, upsetting my ink bottle. Before I could move, the dark blue liquid ran all over my paper and down onto my lap. With a wail I leaped up. "Oh-h -h -! My new dress!" Ink dripped from the wide hem as tears fell onto my cheeks.

Betsy jumped up and embraced me.

"Donald, you owe Amy an apology," said Miss Peterson as she hurried over with towels. She and Betsy started to mop up the ink as well as they could.

"S-o-r-r-y, crybaby," said Donald. "Don't worry. Your parents will get you a new one; you always have new clothes."

I was sorry to hear that Donald hadn't changed much.

"Donald!" Miss Peterson spoke sternly. "Go into the cloakroom immediately. I'll have a talk with your mother later."

She and Betsy finished cleaning up the liquid, but there was a blue stain on the floor for the duration of the year. Of course, my new dress was ruined. I felt bad about that, because I knew Mother worked hard to make my dresses look just so. She never got a chance to let the hem down on this one. Mother made many dresses for me, most of which I wore until I outgrew. That was the only dress I wore just once.

But it was such a pleasant thing to have Betsy spontaneously jump up to comfort me through an embarrassing incident. I never knew the benefits of friendship like this before.

Sixteen

An Unexpected Loss

Ring-*aling-aling...ring*. The telephone on the wall sounded our ring on the party line. One long, one short.

"Oh, pshaw," Mother exclaimed. "That's Tom Swenson wanting my order."

Mother gently scolded herself for not having her list ready. She would apologize and call him back later. Right now she was mixing her "sunshine cake" for tomorrow's Sunday dinner. Because the summer morning was unusually warm, suggesting that by afternoon we'd be sweltering, Mother was hoping to turn off the hot oven as soon as possible.

She answered the phone. "Hello, Tom. I'm sorry, I don't have my order ready. I'll call you back in a little while. All right. Good-bye." Mother replaced the earpiece in its hook on the side of the phone.

Swenson's General Store was not only a place to buy a few groceries but also to catch up on the latest news. It was where farmers exchanged ideas and shook their heads over the prolonged downturn in the local economy. They sat on old wooden chairs, leaning back on two legs against wooden barrels and display cases, and talked around their trademark toothpicks of straw.

It was 1934, and I was thirteen. The Great Depression was in full swing. Swenson's store was not doing well, not only because people were "tightening their belts," as I heard one man say, but more and more people seemed to be buying their needs from larger outfits where prices were a few cents less. To keep his name before the public, Mr. Swenson had recently come up with the idea of calling people for orders. "It's for customer convenience," he said.

I finished the breakfast dishes and began my Saturday cleaning chores while Mother readied her cake for the oven. As I dusted the furniture in the living room and dining room, I heard the telephone ring three times for various other parties in the area.

Running my dusting cloth over the dining chairs, I reminisced about my early visits to Swenson's store, especially the wonderful agony of deciding which kinds of candy to buy with my nickel. I wondered how many fingerprints I'd left on Tom's glass display case. A lot of candy could be bought for five cents. I'd walk out of the store with my little sack fairly bulging with peppermints, root beer barrels, and red hots. As I grew older, what was most special about the store were my visits with Mrs. Swenson.

Within about twenty minutes, Mother had completed mixing up the cake and written her list. But before she was able to call the store, the telephone rang again, this time sounding one very long ring. I heard Mother's startled voice. "It's the emergency ring!"

I ran into the kitchen. Mother lifted the receiver and gasped. Standing close to her, I could hear commotion and a faraway scream.

"What's happened?" Mother insisted, trying to make sense of all the party-line talk. Then with a look of shock, she gasped and leaned into the wall, color draining from her face. "It's Tom Swenson," she said to me.

I was stunned.

Strong woman that she was, Mother gathered her wits about her and again spoke into the phone, this time with authority. "Agnes, Agnes. Listen to me. This is Ida Nesbitt. Try to get hold of yourself." She spoke loudly to be heard over the excited voices of the entire neighborhood. "Tell me what happened....Did you say he shot himself? But, but...I just talked to Tom an hour ago. Was it an accident? Is he alive?"

Mother listened a moment.

"Agnes. Tell me, where is Tom now? In the storeroom? Yes, yes, I'll try to get a call through to Dr. Morse. I'm sure he'll be there as fast as possible. And John will come, too."

Turning to me, she said, "Amy, run and get Dad. Tell him Tom Swenson shot himself."

I flew out the door, across the yard, and jerked open the latch on the pasture gate. In my haste, my shirt caught on the wire fence. I quickly freed it and ran across the pasture to the barn, where Dad and Walter were working. I could feel sweat running down my forehead and back.

"Dad, Dad," I yelled and saw him appear in the doorway. "Tom Swenson shot himself. Mother says to come right away."

Dad stood for a startled instant in disbelief. Then, leaning his pitchfork against the wall, he headed with long strides toward the house. He didn't say a word, but his face looked grave. I had to run to keep up with him.

Mother quickly told Dad the little she knew. "Dr. Morse is on his way," she added. "And I told Agnes you'd come. I'll walk over when I take the cake out of the oven in about 20 minutes."

"Please let me go with you, Dad," I begged, nearly in tears. "Mrs. Swenson is my Adoption Club friend. I want to be with her."

"Okay, but don't rush in. Just follow me."

A few other cars were parked in front of the store. Dad pointed out Dr. Morse's car, saying he must have been close by. When we entered, I stayed a step behind Dad, as he had instructed. A few silent men were standing in the middle of the store, their hands hanging down helplessly. No one sat in the chairs today.

Also in the group was Ned Carlson, Agnes Swenson's twenty-five-year-old nephew who had come from the East to work as a farmhand for the summer, though I heard he'd been unable to find someone who could hire him.

"Doc Morse is back there in the storeroom with Tom," one of the farmers said in a hoarse voice to Dad.

"Tom's not the first to panic over a dying business," another farmer said. "Ever since Black Friday in October of '29, when the stock market crashed, I've heared quite a few men've committed suicide when they lost everything."

"How many more will we lose?" another man wondered.

I inquired where Mrs. Swenson was.

"Agnes? She's upstairs with some of the womenfolk."

Dad nodded at me that I could go up. I climbed the familiar steps, this time with foreboding. The first thing I saw was my friend's knitting basket beside the footstool where I often sat. Agnes was slumped in a rocker with her head in her hands. Two neighbor women, in chairs pulled up close, were comforting her.

Suddenly I froze. What could I do to take away my good friend's pain? I felt as if in a detached stupor, observing the scene from the outside. Mrs. Swenson's insightful words had often encouraged me; now I had none for her. I experienced loss myself, but never because of death. This was something new I didn't understand. I slowly sat down at her feet and lightly put one hand in her lap. She looked up. Her face wet and drawn, she stroked my hand.

"Amy..." was all she said.

In the adjacent small kitchen, two women were busy finishing up some layer cakes and pies that evidently had been ordered by customers for today. "Amy, you can help. Could you spread this white icing on the last chocolate cake?" a woman named Nell asked. "The best way we can help Agnes right now is to finish up these orders."

I was glad to be useful. I was also grateful to have learned some cooking and baking skills from Mother. *Lord, help me to do this job well,* I silently prayed. This was my first experience helping neighbors and friends in the midst of a crisis.

At that moment Ned Carlson came up the stairs and went directly over to his aunt. He knelt and gathered her in his arms. "The doctor's pronounced him dead," he said quietly.

"No!" Her eyes brimming with tears, she looked past all of us. Then, as her glance darted around the room, she despaired, "Tom had been depressed. He'd worked so hard to make something of this store. To see it fail was more than he could bear." She buried her head in Ned's shoulder.

I quickly notified Dad that I was going to stay and help for awhile and would walk home. Mother arrived soon and joined the other women in the kitchen. We both helped ice cakes, which was no trouble, other than the icing tended to slip and slide a bit in the heat. The ladies in the kitchen seemed satisfied with my work. When there was nothing more for me to do, I gave my dear, newly widowed friend a hug and told Mother I would see her at home.

The glaring sun was hot as I trudged along the road and then up the dusty driveway to the house. I didn't feel like going inside yet. Instead I went to a favorite place under the weeping willow tree in the side yard. It wasn't much cooler even in the shade. I lay down in the grass for a talk with my Abba Father.

"Mrs. Swenson taught me that You're always with me. That's good, because I need You now. Even though You gave me a mother and dad who love me, and even though I know You love me, right now I feel so lonely . . . and sad." Tears came. "I love Mrs. Swenson so much, and I know that she loved her husband. Why did Mr. Swenson have to die? Why did he have to leave her? What will she do without her husband to run the store?" I could not sort out my emotions enough to go on. I rolled over in the grass and cried from somewhere very deep within.

I fell asleep, perhaps for mere minutes, and awoke feeling better, almost refreshed. I knew God had been my comforter.

"Thank You, Abba Father."

Within a year, Mrs. Swenson closed the store and moved back East to be near her daughter and son. I dearly missed my visits with her. She had launched me into The Adoption Club, and with it had come my fledgling understanding of spiritual things. But with her absence, as time went by, gloomy thoughts began to blot out what had once been new joy within me. Too many people had been taken away from me during my life. Instead of rejoicing in God's constant love, and growing in appreciation for my adoptive parents, old insecurities of childhood abandonment intensified.

Seventeen

Becoming Mrs. Palmer

Several years went by that seemed in some ways to be replays of those past. There were school days, relieved by summers, then more school days. As I grew older, I had more responsibilities around the house and farm, Betsy and I remained best of friends, and holidays were regularly celebrated in traditional ways.

When I was fifteen, Mother and I took a special trip together to visit one of her aunts and several cousins. We took the train all the way to Vermont. Eating in the dining car was more practice for me to "eat like a lady," and when we arrived, I sensed I was constantly evaluated, both by Mother and her relatives, according to how much I "acted like a lady." *Evidently, I'm becoming a woman, but not a lady*, I thought.

When I was a junior in high school, Mother and Dad were increasingly concerned about my mediocre grades. I did acceptably well in English and history, but math, which had never made much sense to me, was my downfall. I failed one algebra test after another.

"I'm sure you could do better if you'd just apply yourself," was Mother's frequent comment. She didn't realize I spent hours on algebra, even into the night when she thought I was sleeping.

"You're not living up to your potential," was Dad's comment. Several times, the year before, this was followed by, "Amy, how will you ever succeed in college with grades like these?"

But there had been no mention of college for awhile. I figured they had concluded I would never be college material. An old refrain was stirred up in my mind: *The French sisters would be college bound with straight A's. I must be a huge disappointment.*

Early one chilly morning in April, Betsy was waiting for me on the front steps at school. She looked excited. "I have a note for you!" She handed me a white envelope with my name on it.

"Thanks, Betsy; who's it from? I don't recognize the writing."

Her brown eyes widened. "It's from Ed Palmer! He passes my house almost every day when he delivers butter and eggs to Hall's Mercantile. He stopped and gave it to me yesterday afternoon."

Somewhat stunned and very curious, I slipped the envelope into the back of my history book. There was no time to read it now, which was fine; anticipation could be immensely enjoyable. Betsy and I hurried off to separate classes, our matching pleated skirts swaying back and forth.

For some time I had been noticing the Palmer boys at church. They were all good looking, with jet black hair and dark eyes. The family brought their truck to church, the older boys riding in the back. Ed, next to the oldest, was 19 and had graduated last spring. He certainly looked strong and muscular, probably from pitching a lot of hay.

It had been by accident that Ed and I had talked briefly after church last Sunday. As Mother and Dad were chatting with friends, I realized I had left my sweater in the pew. I scurried back into the sanctuary and, rounding the corner, almost collided with Ed. Embarrassed, I mumbled something about forgetting my sweater. He walked beside me to the area where I had been sitting, though there seemed to be no need. At that time I fleetingly wondered, *Could he be interested in me?* Now, with a note waiting between pages of my history book, I felt a flutter of excitement preventing any academic concentration.

When the teacher announced we would spend the balance of class time reading the next chapter, I saw my chance for some reading of my own.

Ed wanted to take me home from church next Sunday. He had asked his father for permission to use the family car. I could reply by sending a note through Betsy.

Of course, the invitation pleased me, but at the same time my more negative side suggested, *He probably won't like me after he gets to know me.*

I showed the note to Betsy after class.

"Amy, Ed is so handsome. You're going to accept, aren't you?"

"Well, I hope to. I think my parents will approve. Everyone knows the Palmers, and the whole family seems nice and polite." I told Betsy about my brief encounter with Ed the previous Sunday.

"M-m-m. I think I'll start dropping my sweater near one of the other brothers...maybe Fred." Betsy giggled. "Will your parents care that they come from the river bottoms? They seem pretty poor."

"I don't think so. Mother and Dad have never told me not to associate with people from a different economic level. Besides, Mr. Palmer is an elder at church. I think it'll be okay."

After Mother and Dad discussed my invitation privately, they decided it would be fine if Ed drove me home next Sunday. Not only that, Mother suggested that I might invite him to stay for Sunday dinner. Mother's love for entertaining was fitting right into my own thoughts.

Sunday finally came, promising to be a sunny spring day. I put on my short-sleeved nylon dress with blue irises around its slightly scooped neckline. The skirt seemed to flow just right when I walked. I had started wearing silk hose to church last year. My black Easter pumps were not very comfortable, but looked good. I set out my short spring coat, just in case I needed it, and went to the dressing table mirror again to examine my rosy cheeks, made so by a dab of powder and just a touch of rouge. Now, just one more comb through my wavy hair. Some girls were getting permanent waves these days, but Mother said there was no point for me to do so.

My thoughts were interrupted when Mother called. "Coming!" I said.

The church service seemed interminably long, while the short ride home in the Palmer family car was over in mere minutes. Mother had prepared most of the dinner and had even set the table, in the dining room, before church. As Ed visited with Dad on the front porch, I helped with last-minute preparations.

I could tell Ed was a little nervous during the meal.

Undoubtedly he wasn't used to eating off china plates or drinking water from crystal goblets. It must have seemed pretty quiet in our dining room. I imagined with nine children in his family, the oldest five being boys, mealtime was a spirited scramble for food.

After dinner, Ed politely expressed his appreciation for the meal, and Mother excused us to walk in the yard and enjoy the afternoon sun.

"There sure is a lot of food to eat at your house. It was really fancy and really good. Thank you again, Amy. I don't get a meal like that very often." I couldn't help but notice what a soft, pleasant voice Ed had.

We crossed the grass to sit on the bench near the birdbath. Jack, our collie, who by now was getting pretty old, loped over to us and stretched out at my feet. The surrounding lilacs weren't blooming yet, but I commented they would be soon.

Ed was easy to talk to. We were both relaxed. I asked him questions about what it was like to grow up in a big family. He told me about hunting and fishing adventures with his siblings along the Minnesota River. It sounded like they had a lot of fun. I could tell he highly respected his parents, even though they were quite strict, adhering to Bible principles as scrupulously as possible. He said all the family, even the little ones, gathered around the kitchen table each evening to read the Bible. Everyone who could, read a chapter out loud, and beginning readers were given help. Ed didn't know how many times they had read the entire Bible from cover to cover.

I loved listening to Ed talk. He asked me about things I like to do. I told him that ever since our hired man Walter and his family had moved onto a farm of their own, I tried to help Dad with chores during the summer months as much as possible. "Dad's not getting any younger; I'm glad I can help him out."

We talked all afternoon until it began to get cool.

"I've got to get home to help with chores. Could I see you

again next Sunday?"

Our after-church visits became regular occasions. Soon Mother didn't even ask if Ed would be coming for dinner. He was expected.

When fall came, we began dating on Saturday nights. Sometimes we went to the ice cream parlor in town for a soda, other times we went to the movies, which were just starting to be made with sound. Ed couldn't afford a soda and a movie on the same night, even though both of them cost just a few cents. I didn't care what we did; I just enjoyed being with Ed.

All summer Ed never suggested that we go to his house. I knew it must be because he came from poor circumstances. Then one warm fall day he said, "Would you like to go for a boat ride?" I knew that meant going to his house, which was near the river.

"Sure. But I've never been in a boat, and I can't swim, so I'll be a little afraid."

"You can't swim?" Ed asked in amazement.

The Palmer children seemed to have grown up swimming. Ed had stories of daring each other to dive off the ice in early spring to see who was going to be the first in for the year.

I met all of Ed's family at church, and it turned out that going to their home was quite pleasant because everyone made me feel welcome. Although the house was smaller than ours and had few luxuries, it was as neat as any house could be with a large family. All the children had chores inside and out; older children helped tend the younger. Although Mr. Palmer had sort of a stern demeanor, Ed always spoke highly of him, so I knew I could be at ease.

The ingenious brothers had rigged up a car engine to power a good-sized wooden fishing boat. I was dubious at first, because of my lack of experience with such things, but Ed took me for some slow rides first until I was comfortable. It wasn't long before we were bouncing along at greater speed, me sitting alongside Ed as he pulled two or three of his siblings behind on a tractor inner tube. When he turned the boat, the inner tube would go flying in a great arc. What a lot of laughter and fun we had.

When Ed and I were apart, all I could think of was him. (This probably did further damage to my grade point average.) I'd almost count the hours until Saturday night. When we were together, I was never happier. *I guess this is love.* The thought frightened me. Love represented danger—danger of losing someone. For this reason, with great willpower, I kept my feelings in check, trying not to reveal to Ed how much I cared about him.

When Ed told me I looked pretty, I wanted to believe him. But somehow I couldn't. No one had ever told me I was pretty. I told him that a teacher long ago said I looked like Amelia Earhart. When I showed him her picture, he said he saw the resemblance, but I was prettier. That night, when I looked in the mirror, I knew I wasn't as pretty as two French sisters I had seen in another picture.

It had been clear for some time that I would not be going to college. My guilt about not measuring up to expectations rose to new heights when high school graduation was a few months off. What did girls do who didn't go to college? It seemed they generally got married. I started thinking seriously about what it would be like to be married to Ed.

Our conversations became more serious. Ed liked farming with his dad, even though most years it was hard to eek out enough to make their marshy acreage profitable. With five older boys, Mr. Palmer had more than enough help. If Ed left home, there would be one less mouth to feed. Maybe marriage was just the answer for both of us.

So, when Ed asked me to marry him, I quickly said yes. Mother and Dad were not particularly happy to have me marry at age eighteen, but they did like Ed. Because he was from a hard-working, respectable family, they agreed.

The wedding took place shortly after graduation, and suddenly, we became Mr. and Mrs. Edward Palmer.

The transition into married life was made somewhat easier because Ed and I moved into the farmhouse where Walter and his family had once lived. Ed became Dad's new hired man, and they got along very well. Ed enjoyed Dad's mild temperament, a contrast to Mr. Palmer's more stern nature, and he proved himself by being a conscientious worker.

One year after we were married, I gave birth to beautiful John David Palmer, named after our two fathers. We all set about adjusting to changes and new responsibilities that come with a baby. Ed and I were thrilled to be parents. Mother and Dad embraced their new position as grandparents, especially Mother, who became the best grandmother her little Johnnie, or any child, could ever ask for.

Then our almost perfect lives changed drastically. When John was six months old, Dad became ill. The doctor told us it was cancer, and Dad wouldn't last long.

I was furious. "Come on God," I railed, shaking my fist at the sky. "Dad never hurt a soul in his whole life. Remember, I've only had a dad for a few years because I never even knew my real father. It's not fair to take him away. I lost my real mother, and then my brother. Then Mrs. Swenson left me. She said You'd always be with me...have You left, too? God, please, don't take Dad. How can You let another person abandon me? Did You give Dad to me just to take him away?"

Within a few weeks, Dad was gone.

My faith in God plummeted. For months I wouldn't talk to Him. Instead, I dwelt on a great and overwhelming fear: *Would Ed leave me, too?*

Eighteen

A Living Faith

After Dad's death, Mother didn't like living alone in her big house. Within a short time, she asked if Ed and I and baby Johnnie (everyone else called him John), would like to move in with her. Ed and I talked it over. Coming from a big family, he was pleased with the idea of living with Mother and sharing her larger house. I wondered how many children he envisioned filling the rooms.

Ed set in motion his natural skills in carpentry, while at the same time running the farm, and within a few months, he had remodeled the attic to include three bedrooms and a bathroom for our little family. But the family didn't stay little for long. Within the next three and a half years we added two adorable girls—Rebecca, whom we called Becky, and Esther. Our attic rooms suited us well. Eventually, John had one of the bedrooms, while Becky and Esther shared the third.

About the time we were getting settled in Mother's house, our faithful old dog, Jack, died. He had been moving slowly for some time, so it probably was a blessing, but Mother and I were especially sad. As Ed buried him under the lilac bushes, I recalled how the day I first arrived at the farm Jack had given me a face lick welcome. We would miss our collie.

Mother loved the children, and they adored her. As time

went by, Mother allowed me to take over more and more of the cooking and housework, while she rocked her precious grandchildren, reading stories, playing games, and singing songs. As they grew older, I saw her face glow with happiness as she watched them cavort in the grass and pump the swing Dad had put up for me years before.

I observed that Mother had learned a lot while raising me. By the time John, Becky, and Esther all appeared on the scene, she had mellowed. Still, as she adored them, and showed affection in ways I had not known, she maintained her position as matriarch, and they respected her as such. Along with her new, playful ways, she managed to more gently instill into the next generation all the rules of etiquette that had defined a great deal of my upbringing.

Seeing Mother enjoy the children was heartwarming in another way. My belief that I was never pleasing enough to her and Dad had nagged at me ever since I had become their daughter. This feeling had greatly intensified when I learned about the French sisters, imagining them to be more accomplished than I ever would be. Now, as I saw Mother's pleasure with my children, I realized that I had given her a great gift, and perhaps I, like her grandchildren, had found a special place of approval in her heart. My relationship with Mother was strengthened by this realization, but there was another relationship I was still ignoring. That one was with God.

From my first acquaintance with Ed, and on into our married life, I was continually impressed by his many admirable qualities. One day, when I was pregnant with John, I went to the barn to retrieve a bucket I had left there. Ed was changing a tire on the tractor. It looked like a big job, and I stopped to watch my able man work. Suddenly, his wrench slipped, hitting his thumb; it obviously hurt.

"Praise the Lord," he said as he shook his hand, his face

turning red.

After the pain diminished, I said, "Ed, I've never heard you swear. How do you control your words, even when you get hurt?"

He thought a moment. "I guess it's because we kids were never allowed to swear growing up. Swearing generally uses God's name in vain, and blames Him for things that happen. It's better to praise Him, because no matter what happens, He is still good." He continued to tighten the lug nuts on the tractor wheel. "If I use God's name in vain (here he interrupted himself to grunt a little, like men do when they're working hard) it invites the enemy to get a foot in the door. Then, pretty soon, he'd try to get a bigger chunk of my life."

I knew when Ed used the word *enemy*, he was referring to Satan. This had become a spiritual conversation, something I had tried to avoid, along with ignoring God, since Mr. Swenson's unfortunate death. But this day, my love and admiration for Ed spurred me on.

"I've never even see you upset or angry," I said.

Again Ed considered his words before he spoke. "Do you know about the fruit of the Spirit?"

"No."

He set his wrench on top of the huge tire. "Well, you know the Bible was pumped into me since I was little. We not only had to memorize verses, but Father made sure we lived them. No fighting or harsh words were allowed. We learned that the fruits of the spirit are love, joy, peace, patience, kindness, goodness, faithfulness, gentleness, and self-control. Behavior outside of these is not God's will."

As Ed turned back to his work, I realized I had some things to think about. Ed had no quarrels with God, just total acceptance. Why was it different for me?

Another time, on a bitterly cold winter day, Ed was driving us home from church. I sat in front, and Grandma was in back holding baby John. All of a sudden the driver's window dropped down and cold air came rushing in.

"Well, shucks," said Ed.

"What do you mean 'shucks'? It's freezing in here! Roll up the window," I shouted.

The baby began to cry.

"I can't roll up the window. The handle must be broken," said Ed calmly. "I'll have to work on it when we get home."

I drew my coat more tightly around me and suffered in silence.

After our Sunday dinner, Ed skillfully fixed the window in his characteristic, unruffled manner. I watched him through the kitchen window, out in the driveway in the cold. Again, like so many times before, I admired Ed's peace and patience. I mulled over his goodness all afternoon. That evening, I decided to ask him about it, knowing his answer would come from the Bible. I was right.

In answer to my inquiry, Ed replied with words of Jesus, *"Peace I leave with you, my peace I give to you; not as the world gives do I give to you. Let not your heart be troubled, neither let it be afraid.'* That's John 14:27."

In the middle of the night, I was still thinking about Ed. *I wonder if I'll ever have his kind of peace.* As I eased into sleep, I found myself murmuring heavenward, "Thank You, God, for giving me such a kind, gentle man."

This was the first time in many months for me to talk to God. It wasn't much of a prayer, but it was the beginning of my walk back to Him, the One I once addressed as "Abba Father."

Being the only man in charge of the Nesbitt farm was a huge

task for Ed. He had never had so many animals or as much acreage to tend, and before we married, he always worked with his capable father and brothers. I watched him learn new management skills with determination and wisdom. Mother took care of the finances and was good at it. When Dad had been gone about two years, she decided to sell off some of the rental property he had acquired and scale back the farm to a more manageable size. Ed and Mother got along well. He always called her "Ma'am," in a most respectful tone, and she obviously was fond of him.

As Ed was learning new things, I was too. I remember when some folks who lived about twenty miles away purchased one of our geldings, Ed agreed to deliver it. Ed said he would need my help loading the young horse into the trailer. Before we ever showed this horse a trailer, it had made up its mind it wasn't going anywhere. First we tried running a long lead line through the trailer. Then coaxing the yearling with carrots, grain, alfalfa. Usually a strap around a horse's rear end would encourage it into a trailer. But not this time.

Ed was sweating, I was dripping, and the horse was also drenched, but after an hour we still had made no progress.

"Let's get the horse in the corner of the fence, then I'll back the trailer into the horse. It can't go anywhere and will have to get into the trailer," Ed schemed.

Wrong. With hindquarters up against the fence, and forced to stand on all four "tiptoes," that horse still would not get into that trailer no matter what we did to "encourage" him.

"I'm almost frustrated," Ed said. "This horse is a dunce."

What an understatement!

I had been "frustrated" for an hour, and could think of a few words stronger than "dunce." Ed "almost frustrated" me too. Why didn't he whip this animal until it understood who was boss?

We left the horse pinned to the fence while we caught our

breath. Leaning against the front of the trailer, I tried to plot our next strategy. But Ed wasn't listening. Instead, I heard him say, "Lord, please help us with this horse." Within seconds, we heard that gelding suddenly leap right in!

I gasped. Ed ran to the back and closed the door, a satisfied smile on his face as he said, "Thank You, Lord." He hopped into the truck. "I'll be heading over to the Holcombs'. Be back in about an hour or so. Thanks for your help, Hon."

Once again Ed hadn't let a situation get the better of him. *He really does put the fruit of the Spirit into action,* I thought. *I wish I could be more like that, especially with the children.* Our third had recently been born. *I let myself get irritated at them, and they aren't nearly as stubborn as that horse! Maybe I need to lean on God for help. I guess I've never really done that.*

I walked across the pasture and sat down on a bale of hay beside the barn. Suddenly, I was ashamed I had neglected God for so long.

"Father God, I need You. Please forgive me for being angry when Dad died." My words faltered, but I pushed myself to continue. "I've been blaming you for what seemed like…more than my share of losses…but You always know what's best. I'll always miss the people I've lost…but You brought Ed to me. I'm learning so much about life and You through Ed. And You've given me three beautiful children. Help me to be thankful for all the good I have, and not dwell on what I don't. I want to be a good mother…and a good wife. It seems like Ed really knows You. I want to know You too, because You are good. Please come back to me."

Ed lived the principles I had heard in sermons since childhood. By his example, without even knowing it, he had led me to reaffirm my faith in God.

We began reading the Bible together each evening after the children were in bed. Then we would pray, asking God to intervene in every part of our lives. My faith grew as we saw

God answer prayers and bless our family.

One night when we were in the book of Romans, Ed was reading, "*For ye have not received the spirit of bondage again to fear, but ye have received...*"

I interrupted, completing the verse, "*...the Spirit of adoption, whereby we cry, Abba, Father!*"

Ed looked surprised.

"I know that verse," I said. "We learned it in Vacation Bible School when I was in fifth grade. That's when I joined The Adoption Club!"

I began to tell Ed all about the day I had agreed in prayer with Mrs. Swenson, asking Jesus to come into my life. "She explained that through Jesus, we can be in God's family. He adopts us and loves us perfectly, forever."

Ed put his arm around me. "I'm so glad your mother and dad adopted you, because that allowed us to meet. But we're both adopted by God, and that's even better."

And He'll never leave us, I said to myself.

Little did I know the verse from Romans would soon put me through another time of testing.

Nineteen

The Adoption Club Grows

America's involvement in World War II increased dramatically. Thousands and thousands of the country's young men had been called to serve in Europe, Asia, and Africa. Many never came back. For some time I thought, *Surely, Ed a father of three with a big farm to keep up, will not have to go.* But he was drafted into the United States Army in March of 1944. "I love my country," he said. "God has made it great, and I have a responsibility to defend it...for you and our family."

Ed was sent to boot camp in Texas, then deployed to the Philippine Islands. He faithfully wrote us encouraging letters, only sometimes including details of difficulties his unit faced. "It's so humid here we always drip with sweat and our clothes are never dry. No running water or electricity is one thing, but trying to survive with all the bugs is even worse. The mosquitoes swarm around our eyes, and our lips are swollen from bites." I knew there were things he was dealing with much worse than weather and bugs.

Throughout the long months Ed was gone, I repeated over and over, *Abba Father, I'm yours. Keep me from the bondage of fear.* Daily I reminded myself that because of our adoption into God's family, both Ed and I were his children. No matter what happened, our heavenly Father would take care of us.

As Ed's letters continued, I could tell he was leaning on

God for his very survival. He began to include a spiritual teaching in each letter. Sometimes I didn't know if they were more for himself, or for his family back home. *The Lord disciplines those he loves,* Ed wrote. *God's children often undergo extra training and discipline in order to fit them for their high destiny.*

Mother and I became closer than we ever had been as we cared for the children and home together. She and I huddled close to the radio each evening for news of the war. She was a strong woman, and I appreciated her presence.

Once a day we gathered up the three children and prayed for Ed and all those serving our nation. Mother usually held Becky on her lap, with one arm around John as he stood close at her side. I would hold little Esther. We often ended the prayer time by quoting part of Psalm 91. *"For He shall give His angels charge over you, to keep you in all your ways. In their hands they shall bear you up, lest you dash your foot against a stone."*

Seven-year-old John was always full of questions now. After hearing us repeat these words several times, he began saying them with us, then asking for clarification.

"Grandma, does Daddy have an angel with him?"

"Grandma, does Daddy's foot hurt?"

Mother and I would try to answer his questions as best we could, and reassure him of God's loving care for his soldier father, as well as us at home.

The two of us couldn't care for the livestock, so the cows and horses were sold. The barns would have to sit empty for awhile. Uncle Knute offered to plant our corn, but that crop was all he could help with and keep his own farm going too. Burton had enlisted in the Navy at the start of the war, so Uncle Knute and Aunt Annie were alone.

One June afternoon, I was thrilled to see Betsy step out of a roadster in our driveway and come to the door. I had rarely seen her since she had become a teacher the previous fall at a school about fifteen miles away. I was hoping she would be more available this summer. With Ed gone, I was lonesome for my old friend.

Mother and the children were napping. Over cups of freshly brewed tea, Betsy and I had a grand time catching up on news. After sharing bits of Ed's latest letters, we moved on to Betsy's school year that had been everything she had expected—many joys with lots of work.

With a slight blush, Betsy told me she had begun a friendship with a young man she met in teachers' college. "His name is Carl. He's pretty dreamy, Amy, and I think he's really serious about me." Then she stopped, her big eyes misting over. "Last week he enlisted. There has been a partial freeze on drafting teachers…but he thought the war effort needed him more than the classroom."

I sympathized. It was hard to be a man in wartime, and in a different way, hard to be left at home. Our talk turned to other differences the war had made in our lives.

"I sure miss having silk stockings," Betsy bemoaned. "But I guess that's nothing really important."

I chimed in, "I can't wait to be able to buy all the sugar I want. Can you imagine Mother trying to make her wonderful peach and apple pies without sugar!" Then I felt a twinge of guilt at even mentioning it. "If our troops need the sugar, I want them to have it all."

"Amy, I was looking forward to seeing you a lot over the

summer. But I've decided to work in the munitions plant in St. Paul for three months. With so many men bravely fighting...and Carl too... it's the least I can do."

How excited we were when we heard over the radio in August of 1945 that the Japanese had surrendered, but crestfallen when Ed wrote he wouldn't be able to return home until November. I continued my anxious daily wait for the mailman. Now he had a little more time to write, so we sometimes received multiple letters in a week. Often there were personal messages to one or more of us. With each letter's arrival, I excitedly summoned our little troop. John would take up the call, "It's a letter from Daddy!" and the children gathered around Mother's and my feet like baby chicks to hear me read. When there were special words for John and Becky, they lit up like Christmas trees. Sometimes I saved Ed's devotional words for just Mother and me before we went to bed. His letters were so precious. I often held them in my hand all through the night.

Ed often mentioned the orphaned Philippine children that gathered around his camp. Some were abandoned by GI fathers; others had lost both parents to death. All were victims of war. To survive, Ed wrote, hundreds, perhaps thousands, of these children became street smart beggars.

They call all the GI's "Joe."

"Hey, Joe, can you spare a dime?" and "Come on, Joe, got some candy?" These children know when it's our mealtime. They come out of nowhere, sit close by, and watch us eat. Of course, we can't enjoy our chow with all those big brown eyes staring at us. We always end up

giving away a good portion of our rations. In fact I'm losing weight—can't wait to get home to some home cooking by my ladies on the farm.

Another letter said:

We have to watch our stuff like a hawk because the older kids on the street pick pockets and steal whatever is lying around if we're not watching.

Stories about these unfortunate children touched our hearts. We began to include them in our prayers as Ed's letters seemed to dwell more and more on them. For some time, we had been sending "care packages" to Ed about every two weeks with cookies, and hard candies. We weren't surprised when he told us he was giving our "goodies" away to the orphaned children. In our next package, we included chewing gum, jump ropes, several small rubber balls, and a couple stuffed toys.

Ed expressed his pleasure with the package: *It was hard to decide which children to give things to.*

Shortly after that he wrote:

I want to tell you about one little tyke in particular. Her name is Maria, and she's about a year old. A twelve-year-old girl named Daisy carries her around. Their families had lived next door to each other until a bomb fell on their houses, killing the parents.

Ed's next letter ushered in a significant change to our family.

Dearest Family,
I am well and pray the same for each of you every day. It won't be long now before we're back together again. I can

hardly wait.

There is something very serious I would like you to consider. I had a conversation with Daisy today. She begged me to take Maria home with me. She said, "Maria have better life in America." I explained that I already have a family. Then she said, "Joe, I can't take more care of Maria."

Amy, kids, Mother, I don't think I can leave this darling, helpless little girl behind. Some of the older children might make it somehow, but Maria is too little. When I look into her eyes, my heart breaks. So, I'm asking you all from the bottom of my heart, will you join together on your side of the world and pray about adopting her into our family? I will be praying also, way over here across the ocean. I'm sure God will give us the same answer.

We all love each other so much. I'm sure there is enough love for one more. The government doesn't know what to do with all these orphans and is making it fairly easy for GIs to adopt them, but I don't know how long that will last.

If she is going to be ours, please let me know as soon as possible so I can start the paperwork.

By the way, there's a verse in the Bible that says, "God puts the lonely in families." Just thought I'd mention that.

Your loving husband, father, and son,
Ed

Mother and I sat for a moment completely stunned. Then I looked into the eyes of each dear one around me—first Johnnie, the talkative little "man of the house," then Becky, our shy, affectionate one, and Esther, joyful toddler, and finally…my dear mother, who had become the ultimate grandmother. How could I deny a child, a child who had obviously stolen my husband's heart, access to this fold?

Mother and I smiled at each other. There was a silent recognition that God had already prepared our hearts for His will. As joy welled up, we both started to laugh. God was good! Ed was coming home, and with him would be a child who needed a family. The children, without understanding why we were so giddy, but sensing it was something good, joined our mirth. We all laughed and giggled until tears rolled down Mother's and my cheeks.

I hugged Mom as she said, "It'll be wonderful to have another little one! Esther is already twenty-six months old. She needs a younger sister. I wonder if there's space in the girls' room to squeeze in another crib. And, Amy, I think I better start on another quilt...."

The four months until Ed came home seemed like a lifetime. But it allowed us to prepare for Maria by sorting through things that could be reused from Becky and Esther, and making or buying other special items just for her. Then, as I recalled scenes from my own adoption, I realized this was an important time of preparation in other ways. Fitting into a family doesn't just happen because of good intentions. It's more complicated than that as both child and new parents blend their diverse experiences, personalities, and expectations. Because Maria was from a different culture, what adjustments would this require of her and us beyond my own experience? What would it take to help Maria become part of us, and we part of her?

Then one day I picked up my open Bible from a table where I had laid it earlier. My eyes focused on a verse I had never noticed before. *"The stranger that dwelleth with you shall be unto you as one born among you, and thou shalt love him as thyself; for ye were strangers in the land...."*

God was directing this verse to me. It was a command coupled with comfort. We were to love Maria no matter what, just like Mother and Dad had loved me. Even as it must have been difficult for them to include a "stranger" in their home who had no knowledge of how to be part of a family, under God's instruction and help, we would do the same for Maria.

I was prompted to spend more time with seven-year-old John. When the younger children were napping, I began to familiarize him with my children's Bible story book that had delighted Betsy and me years before. As I showed him the pictures, I told him the stories in simple language a seven-year old would understand. In particular, I told him about baby Moses, and Queen Esther, and young Samuel, and how God had planned that they would live most of their lives apart from their birth parents. John too was getting ready for Maria.

On the windy November day when Ed finally arrived, bearing his precious bundle, our enthusiastic hugs practically knocked him over in the doorway. Everyone talked at once, clamoring for his attention. John and Becky jumped up and down with squeals. Esther, who was only six months old when Ed left and could not even distinctly remember her dad, joined right in the riotous scene. Mother, Ed, and I did not try to contain our happy tears.

Poor little Maria was alarmed at the commotion. She turned her head into Ed's shoulder and began to whimper.

"Oh, Ed, she's so beautiful. She's so tiny." I held out my arms. "Will you come to your new mommy?"

Of course she clung to Ed, the only familiar person in the room. But Grandma had the touch. Just as the other children had found comfort in their grandmother's lap, it wasn't long before Maria was content, rocking back and forth, lulled by Mother's soft humming.

Ed sank into a chair, as the three children continued to compete for his attention. John made sure Ed noticed his Army uniform, sized for his little-boy frame. "It's just like yours, Daddy! I'm a soldier too!" From his chair, Ed smiled and saluted his son. Becky, who had just turned five, insisted that Daddy inspect her favorite doll. Two-year-old Esther flitted around the room singing, "Daddy, watch me…watch me…I butterfly!"

I was afraid the chaos was overwhelming him. Anyone would be exhausted after such long trip home, and the children had grown and changed so much in his absence he could hardly take it all in. I embraced him one more time and set about to distract the children from the kitchen, promising to come right back to make a fresh pot of coffee.

Ed was the first person in my life who left me but returned. My husband had come home. *Praise You, Father God.*

The following day, Ed said he noticed a difference in me. "And it's not only that you look prettier than ever, Amy," he said as he pulled me close.

I felt myself blush, but I was pleased.

"I'm so proud of you, how you've kept the family together, everyone so happy and healthy. I know it wasn't easy to be here without a man on the farm. There's a new strength about you, a new peace."

"I'm so glad you're home, Ed. I love you so much."

Ed was right. In his absence, I had felt strength and peace almost every day. Best of all, God had kept me from fear.

"I had plenty of lonesome times," I assured him, "but I was determined to lean on Abba Father, like I knew you were depending on Him in the middle of war."

"It's funny, about war." Ed said thoughtfully. "War is all about death. But God…God can bring life, even out of war. He's amazing."

I knew he was referring to his encounter with Maria. "Oh, Ed. Thank you for being so in tune with God that you would rescue this little one and bring her home so she can have a new life." I hugged him more tightly.

"On the long trip home, I was thinking about what you called 'The Adoption Club,'" Ed said. "I look forward to the day when our children are individually old enough to understand, and will be welcomed into that forever club."

"And, just like for me, it will be Maria's second adoption," I added.

We looked at each other and smiled. Nothing else needed to be said. The Adoption Club had gone full circle.

About the Author

BARBARA SCOTT and her husband, Gary, reside in Redmond, Washington. Married for 36 years, they have two grown sons, a daughter-in-law, and two grandchildren. In her first book, *From Rubble to Restoration,* Barbara tells the dramatic story of their family's terrible undoing and divinely orchestrated reconstruction.

For the past eight years, the Scotts have served with Youth With A Mission (YWAM) at their headquarters and flagship campus at the University of the Nations (UofN) in Kona, Hawaii. They have traveled extensively in the Philippines, Korea, and Thailand, speaking in churches, YWAM bases, and other ministries. While in Kona, Barbara wrote many articles for YWAM's web site and UofN's *Transformations* magazine.

Her short story, "She Pierced My Heart," is featured in Dr. Gary Chapman's book: *Love is a Verb: Stories of what happens when love comes alive* (Bethany, 2009).

Barbara's passion is to inspire others through her writing to find God and experience His ability to work all things together for good.

www.oaktara.com